PENGUIN BOOKS

# TWENTY AFTER MIDNIGHT

Daniel Galera is a Brazilian writer and translator. He was born in São Paulo but lives in Porto Alegre, where he has spent most of his life. He has published five novels in Brazil to great acclaim, including *The Shape of Bones* and *Blood-Drenched Beard*, which was awarded the 2013 São Paulo Literature Prize. In 2013, *Granta* named Galera one of the Best of Young Brazilian Novelists, and in 2017 he was chosen by *Freeman's* as one of the international authors representing the future of new writing. He has translated the work of Zadie Smith, John Cheever, and David Mitchell into Portuguese.

# TWENTY AFTER MIDNIGHT

a novel

DANIEL GALERA

TRANSLATED BY JULIA SANCHES

PENGUIN BOOKS

PENGUIN BOOKS
An imprint of Penguin Random House LLC
penguinrandomhouse.com



Originally published in Portuguese under the title
*Meia-noite e vinte* by Companhia das Letras, São Paulo.
An English translated excerpt of this work, by Eric M. B. Becker,
was featured in *Freeman's: The Future of New Writing*, 2017.

LIBRARY OF CONGRESS CATALOGING-IN-PUBLICATION DATA

Names: Galera, Daniel, 1979– author. | Sanches, Julia, translator.
Title: Twenty after midnight : a novel / Daniel Galera ; translated by Julia Sanches.
Other titles: Meia-noite e vinte. English
Description: [New York] : Penguin Books, [2020] | Originally published in Portuguese under the title Meia-noite e vinte by Companhia das Letras, São Paulo.
Identifiers: LCCN 2019034210 (print) | LCCN 2019034211 (ebook) |
ISBN 9780735224797 (paperback) | ISBN 9780735224780 (ebook)
Classification: LCC PQ9698.417.A4 M4513 2020 (print) |
LCC PQ9698.417.A4 (ebook) | DDC 869.3/5—dc23
LC record available at https://lccn.loc.gov/2019034210
LC ebook record available at https://lccn.loc.gov/2019034211

Printed in the United States of America
1 3 5 7 9 10 8 6 4 2

BOOK DESIGN BY LUCIA BERNARD

# TWENTY AFTER MIDNIGHT

My sudden urge to accelerate the world's destruction was connected in a way to the human shit stinking up the sidewalks and the fumes wafting from the slime pooled around the city's dumpsters, to the bus strike and the widespread despair over the late January heat smothering Porto Alegre, but, if there was a before and an after, a line that separated the life I thought I'd have from the life I ended up having, this line was the news of Andrei's death the night before, when he was robbed at gunpoint near Hospital de Clínicas, just a few blocks from the Ramiro Barcelos neighborhood where I was walking. I had stopped so abruptly while trying to process that piece of information on my Twitter feed that my right foot, wet with sweat, had slipped in its sandal and my ankle had twisted, sending me crashing onto the hot sidewalk, my left arm jutting ridiculously into the air to protect my phone.

Near the site of my fall, a homeless woman rummaged through a dumpster, doubled over its edge like an ostrich with its head buried in the sand, black legs and bare feet poking out from her pink pleated dress. Hearing me groan, she slipped out of the container's mouth, lowered its lid, and walked toward me. I was already propped up on one of my knees, adjusting the strap on my sandal, when she asked if I was all right and offered to help. Only then did I notice that she was a cross-dresser with fine, curly hair covering her thighs and sculpted arms. I said I was all right, thank you, I just needed to sit down for a second. She watched me with interest as I eased myself onto the nearest stoop and, although she looked like she might want to lean over and help, kept a safe distance. Her beautiful face was covered in a thick icing of grease, and her smile, filled with white, straight teeth, seemed more improbable on her than the women's clothing she wore so naturally. I assured her that I was fine, and she didn't insist. Instead, she headed in the direction of Avenida Osvaldo Aranha, her legs gently crisscrossing, like a girl in a bikini stepping toward the pool at her boyfriend's pal's house.

I moved my ankle around, checking for torn tendons. I was scared to look at my phone again, because doing so would confirm the news that just a few hours earlier, Andrei had been shot by a mugger someplace close to where I sat, and was now dead at the age of thirty-six—so I calculated, remembering he was just three years older than me. The step I had sat on was covered in burned matches, and the thought that they might have been lit by Andrei's murderer, a crack fiend ready to kill for a hit, sent a chill through me, followed by nausea. Pearls of sweat formed behind my ear and ran down my neck. I wondered what had happened to my city while I had been away, which was ridiculous, considering that just minutes earlier it had seemed to me that nothing at all had happened, that it was the same city it'd always been. It was probably then, in those few mystifying moments, that I was struck by the thought that these days were simply the gateway to a slow and irreversible catastrophe, or that the force, the natural law or entity, that gave life to our expectations—and by "our," I mean my expectations, those of my friends, my generation—was starting to die out.

It was my first trip to Porto Alegre in almost two years. I had arrived a week earlier, filled with memories of a breezy, colorful town trapped in the amber of spring days tinted by blue skies and the flowering pink trumpet trees of Parque da Redenção, memories that were undoubtedly real and yet pointed to a past both indistinct and disconnected from the present. Throughout that week, the city, carpeted in filth and sizzling under the heat of the worst summer in decades, had reminded me of a hepatitis patient left to die in the sun. Cars and people steered clear of the streets on that final day of January, school vacation in full swing and Carnaval just around the corner, and the municipal transport strike, which was on the fifth consecutive day of its shutdown, was the final component in a bell jar of lethargy that had descended over everything. Workers in the city's outskirts cried into news cameras that they couldn't get to work and their bosses were docking their pay. Jitneys, school vehicles authorized by the city for emergency use, and illegal buses that seemed like they might fall to pieces at any moment sped down empty bus lanes crammed with heat-stricken passengers. Cabbies honked their horns and wreaked havoc willy-nilly, high on the overdose of passengers, some even charging night fares in the light of day just because they could.

The cabdriver who, a few days earlier, had driven me from the airport to the hospital where my dad was admitted said the strike had already been deemed illegal by the Labor Courts, but that the strikers were unmoved and there was no end in sight. Buses seen daring to leave their garages were pummeled with rocks by trade unionists. Drivers quarreled with each other and with their bosses, who were being accused of encouraging this stoppage as a way of pressuring the government to raise fares, even though it wouldn't, not in the wake of the June 2013 protests that, fueled by police violence, had put an end to countrywide fare hikes. In the meantime, plants scorched under the sun, the real feel in the early morning resembled a rain forest, and all over downtown, temperature displays showed afternoon highs of over forty-five degrees Celsius. The tap water ran hot. Not warm. Hot. Nearly scalding. Several sections of the city were without power or water, sometimes for hours or even days. Those living in the outskirts had it the worst, of course, and started road blockages to protest this neglect. Panhandlers crowded together in the shade, napping the morning away on their cardboard beds, their sleep incredulous and beggarly, their eyes half-open. All I wanted was to nestle into the building's stoop and sink into that same slumber.

After a slow lull, I glanced again at my cellphone screen, which still displayed the story of Andrei Dukelsky's murder on the *Zero Hora* news site. I scrolled through the article, the sweat from my finger slicking the iPhone glass. According to his girlfriend, a certain Francine Pedroso, Andrei had gone out for a jog around nine thirty that night, taking with him only his house key and his smartphone, which the criminals had swiped. Though the crime scene was in a reasonably busy area, even at night, there had been no witnesses. "One of the most promising new talents of contemporary Brazilian literature," was the descriptor accorded him in the text. "Duke, as his friends called him." The hashtag #RIPDuke offered instant access to the shock and sadness expressed by his friends and readers on social media. I didn't have the guts to click on it.

Andrei and I weren't that close anymore. The last time I'd seen him was a few years earlier in São Paulo, on the evening of his last book signing, or at least the last one I heard about. He had stopped updating Twitter and, as I later found out, had committed Facebook suicide. Our relationship had been at its most intense fifteen years earlier, in college, back when we both wrote for our email fanzine *Orangutan* and had conversations we would later recall as extremely profound. He made me read Camus, João

Gilberto Noll, *Moby-Dick*. I tried to picture where our other e-zine contributors might be, especially Emiliano, who I had missed the most in São Paulo. I remembered meeting Andrei for the first time in the journalism school courtyard, smoking like he'd started lighting up in diapers, sober and burly as a judo fighter, his hairline receding in peaks, signaling the onset of early baldness. He donned high-quality pink and blue shirts and wore blazers to bars, a flamboyant statement for a late-1990s college kid. His nails were always dirty and overgrown, and he stank a little. Duke never ceased to be a mystery to us. Among his friends, but especially us Orangutans, there was a sort of unspoken competition as to who would be the first person to really understand him, to win his trust, become his confidante. But Duke would open up to no one. His novels and short stories proved unhelpful in solving this enigma. Reading him, I felt that there were things that he'd even kept hidden from literature. As if he were awaiting some distant future in which he'd be ready to write about them.

The funeral at the Jewish cemetery on Avenida Oscar Pereira—the article on my phone continued—was for family only. There would be no wake, per Jewish tradition. Sitting there on some apartment building stoop, craving the numb slumber of the homeless, I thought of how Andrei's body had lay strewn on a sidewalk about five hundred meters from where I sat, of how his dried-up blood, spilled over the paving stones, would have left marks that now mixed with remnants of garbage slurry and dog piss, and then I caught myself thinking, against my will, that in truth he'd been spared, that maybe, at the end of the day, he was the lucky one. Because he'd escaped some horrible, fast-approaching thing, which we'd all have to grow used to.

I remembered I had my dad's nicotine patches in my purse. I tried to focus, locked my cell screen, got up, and began walking toward Avenida Ipiranga. A column of black smoke rose from the concrete embankments of Arroio Dilúvio, and crossing the bridge, I spotted two boys in rags squatting by a crackling fire, probably melting down copper cables to sell at the junkyard. The riverbed of the Dilúvio was no more than a stream snaking between sandbanks exposed under the sun, though in the scant deeper pools sluggish fish were visible in the ropy, gray sewage water. On the other side of the avenue, still in the Santana neighborhood, on one of the smaller blocks of Rua Gomes Jardim—lined with verandaed houses partially concealed behind unkempt gardens—and beside a glass store and an old butcher who had frightened me as a little girl, lived my parents, for whom the world, due to matters of health and longevity, was closer to ending than it was for me.

And the world really had nearly ended for my dad. At sixty-six, he'd had a heart attack and was now at home recovering from a heart bypass. Eight days earlier, when my cellphone had awoken me before sunrise in my São Paulo apartment, the surgery, which would last four hours, was already under way. On the other end of the line, my mom had sounded more cross than scared. Dad only shared details of the incident once he was discharged from the ICU and his mind had cleared. After eating a dinner of grilled cheese and salami, brought to our front door by a delivery guy from his favorite diner, and watching TV over two glasses of Campari tonic and cigarettes smoked with his usual abandon, Dad went to bed. He woke up at daybreak with heartburn and mild chest pain, wandered around the living room for a while, and, realizing the pain wasn't passing, decided to swing by the ER. Seeing no reason to disturb my mother's delicate slumber, he climbed into the car and drove himself to Hospital Mãe de Deus, unknowingly suffering a heart attack while smoking Marlboro Lights with his elbow resting on the window and his other hand on the wheel of the automatic Honda Fit, probably listening to some band like Simply Red on Rádio Continental, certain that it was just gas or some other relatively inoffensive thing. As soon as he mentioned his chest pain to the triage doctor, they took his pressure and quickly shepherded him to the cardiologist. Shortly afterward, he was on the operating table.

I arrived at the hospital with luggage in tow and found my dad at the end of his first day post-surgery, hugging his pillow and hocking up pulmonary secretions before my mother's saucer-wide eyes. He was flustered and kept asking if it was day or night. Whenever his blanket was moved for some test or procedure, I was struck by the impossible whiteness of his body and thought to myself that this couldn't possibly be my father's skin tone, that he was much darker. He'd been drained of too many fluids, didn't have enough blood, something wasn't right. I tried not to look at him at length, thinking he felt ashamed of being exposed to me like that. And, for my part, it repulsed me to see him so debilitated. Lying back on his bed at the mercy of probes and needles, his sternum sewn together with steel thread that would remain in his skeleton long after all his other tissues had turned to dust, he was an emblem not only of his own death but of mine. This morbidity stepped into the background the moment he was transferred to a room. He became cheerful and joked that I was free to experiment on his worthless carcass, that it was high time he handed it over to science. I told him that all I needed for my research were *Arabidopsis* and sugarcane seeds, but a friend of mine at the University of São Paulo was studying the effects of cigarettes and cold-cut meats on the bodies of bullheaded old men and that his corpse might, perhaps, be of interest to him. Colleagues from the college prep course and the schools where Dad taught Portuguese Language and Literature, and a trio of doting students, stopped by for a visit. I helped him on strolls down the hospital corridor through which he whined about my mom's recent neuroses, the government's economic interventionism, current laissez-faire pedagogical practices, and his bratty students, who felt they had a right to everything, all the while glancing at me sidelong, trying to gauge my responses to what he said. After five days in the hospital, they let him go home. There, his mood swung out of control. Sometimes he would start crying out of the blue and stare at us, bewildered, claiming not to know why, tears still streaming down his cheeks. He made a point of standing in the shower and tending to his own incisions, fretting over the breathing exercises prescribed by his physiotherapist. He had a long life ahead of him, I thought. Who knew—maybe he'd even come out of all this strong enough to witness the world completely wither away.

On the morning I learned of Andrei's death, I had gone out to buy nicotine patches at my dad's request. He'd asked for a specific brand that was hard to find, and since the buses were out of commission, I'd had to trek all the way to a pharmacy in Bom Fim. By the time I got home, I looked like an Ebola patient. I figured my dad was asleep, left the little bag of nicotine patches on the dining table, and went to the kitchen. I filled a glass with iced tea, added a squeeze of lime and some brown sugar, walked back to the living room, and slumped onto the sofa, smack beneath the AC airstream. The battered old couch had its own special odor, which drowned out the smell of roses and lilies my mom often kept in a vase on the coffee table. I called the scent Dust Mite. Ever since I had learned as a little girl of the existence of dust mites from a magazine article on respiratory illnesses, I'd associated the smell of the sofa with hosts of those diminutive creatures, which I pictured infiltrating the cushions' coarse fabric by the millions. The piece was accompanied by a close-up from an electron microscope that showed dust mites like green olives with tiny legs perched on balls of grayish thread. I must have been nine or ten when I first saw that picture, back when the threat of dust mites had reached domestic-phobia levels in households across Brazil. My parents, following in the steps of almost everybody else, installed air filter machines like tiny tin robots in every room of the house. I pictured dust mites chewed up in a mass genocide by minuscule cogs to the sound of the filters' mechanical humming. Where had all those filters gone? People couldn't care less about mites anymore. "Four pairs of legs and a pair of pedipalps," I whispered under my breath, recalling a section from one of the biology textbooks I'd read and reread in my childhood. It described an attribute of the arachnid, the class that covered mites, spiders, and scorpions. I liked saying it aloud, its near-comic melody bringing to mind a nursery rhyme. Sometimes I caught myself mentally humming the words "four pairs of legs and a pair of pedipalps" as I dried dishes, peed, or sat at my computer hammering away at the unfinished draft of an article.

I said those words over and over like a mantra for a few minutes as I sipped at my iced tea and felt the sweat drying on my cold skin. Andrei, murdered. The anxiety I had just experienced out on the street wasn't waning; instead, I felt it take root in me, incontrovertibly, like soil absorbing poisonous water. I looked at the glass in my hand, pictured it morphed into hundreds of scattered shards, and thought of how there was something perverse and improper about an intact glass, almost as if it were conscious of being a glass, an awareness it certainly didn't deserve. I squeezed the glass tight, both wanting and not wanting to break it, in an urge not unlike that cruel desire people sometimes get to crush a puppy.

Bunking with my parents at the age of thirty-three—even under the circumstances of my dad's near-fatal medical episode—made me feel, predictably, as if I were regressing emotionally. I loved the objects in that house, which didn't stop them from filling me with a certain unease. I glanced at the framed photographs of Tatuíra, our deceased mutt with tiger-striped fur, at the violets sitting in delicate vases by the kitchen's louvre windows, at the collection of cookbooks with half-faded spines, and conjured up the gas-powered shower that spat out air as you tried to bathe, the vast library of books in my dad's office, the reference books my mom would leave stacked up on the floor of the cottage behind the house, where she worked on her illustrations, the guest room with imbecilic artifacts of the time when it had belonged to their only daughter, things such as an *Edward Scissorhands* poster featuring Johnny Depp and Winona Ryder.

The house's familiarity only intensified the fear that I'd demilitarized some faraway strategic front, exposing a flank through which my life could be taken from me. Rent was past due on my São Paulo apartment, more than half the lightbulbs needed replacing, and my research on the circadian rhythms of sugarcane remained stuck in the wreckage from a quarrel that had resulted in my failure to receive my doctorate. The next defense was scheduled for early April, and I'd been careful to secure a date that would force my nemesis, Professor César, to send in a substitute juror. This practically guaranteed I would pass the second examination, and yet the mere thought of the humiliation that nematode had put me through made me quake with anxiety and rage. I was convinced I was a victim of psychological harassment, but I knew it would've been counterproductive to act on that. César could crush me, if he liked.

My fingers gripped the glass so tightly they turned yellow. I asked myself what would happen if I just dropped everything. If I didn't go back. If I disappeared into the forest, fled to Uruguay, and, from there, listened to the distant echoes of civilization's demise. My sense of failure and loss would follow me to my grave. Version one. I'd experience a kind of freedom I could never have imagined existed. Version two. The question was whether, beyond the narrow lens of our vanity, our lives' ambitions really were gratuitous, futile, and easily forgotten, as I sometimes, secretly, suspected.

I relaxed my fingers, swallowed the last ice cube, and set down the glass on the coffee table. I needed to do something to escape this vortex of anxiety. I recalled my favorite way of passing the time in that house, the habit I had acquired as a child of riffling through my mom's illustrated books, among them the volumes on zoology, botany, and anatomy that had fascinated me ever since I was a little girl. I left through the kitchen's back door. The heat outside, even in the seconds it took me to cross the patio to the cottage, was so punishing that I wondered if those conditions might not be hostile to human life. Human fragility really was endearing. Millions of years of evolution that culminated in living beings astonishingly maladapted to the planet's natural environment, as evidenced by our continual suffering at the slightest change in temperature or lack of resources, by our humiliating vulnerability to any kind of atmospheric condition or our exposure to materials and other organisms—not to mention our minds' even more humiliating vulnerability to any old rubbish, to anxiety and hope. We weren't suited to that natural world. It was no surprise we were trying to destroy it.

Fortunately, my mom was working in her studio, the AC on full-blast and the radio tuned as ever to Rádio Itapema, which just then played a Nei Lisboa ballad that, for some reason, took me back to afternoons of drinking with my classmates at bars on Rua Doutor Flores, in the Old Town, after our college prep classes. Her desk was long and bare, with no drawers, just a wooden slab that rested on round metal legs. Her iMac, scanner, and digital drawing tablet were like alien technologies next to her FM radio with its extended antenna. These devices sat beside sheets of paper covered in sketches and various pencil holders filled with pens. She'd been drawing on her computer for years, but I still remembered the pre-digital days, her table always laden with sheets of heavyweight paper in creamy textures, with cases of colored pencils, rulers, styluses, watercolors, and paintbrushes. When I was still a tyke, she'd give me sheets of tracing paper so I could copy book illustrations with 0.5mm archival ink pens. I was terrified of breaking the tips of those pens. Mom specialized in technical and what she referred to as realistic illustrations. With delicate wrist flourishes, she drew hearts and throats for medical textbooks, bowls of milky cereal surrounded by ripe strawberries for boxes of granola, Amazonian birds for trading cards—free gifts tucked into milk chocolate wrappers—and tractors and combine harvesters for agricultural machinery catalogs. All she needed were reference photos. Once, before being driven to school, I had seen one of her illustrations on a bread wrapper at breakfast and asked why they didn't just use photographs instead of drawings so realistic they sometimes seemed like mere copies.

"I don't make photographic copies," she said. "I don't draw things. That's what photos are for. I draw the idea of things. Picture a perfect apple. I draw the thing you're picturing, not the real apple sitting in our fruit bowl."

In most cases, the illustrations were near-identical reproductions of the photo, and though it was difficult to pinpoint what set them apart—as in a game of spot the difference—there was without question something profoundly distinct about those images. More than photographs, her drawings were like statues of saints or Renaissance paintings, full of an idyllic allure that PR agencies, publishers, and other businesses she worked for seemed to grasp far better than I ever had. From an artistic perspective, her illustrations were worthless, subject to the most vulgar ideals of perfection. In some cases, however, when the client's briefing allowed her more freedom or suggested a more unusual approach than was standard, she could create strangely poetic images that were less constrained by labels or catalogs and closer to hyperrealist paintings, where the presence of the technique employed and their almost undetectable anomalies lent expressivity to what might, from afar, pass for a documentary photograph. Among my favorite illustrations was a piece she herself was proud of, to the point she'd framed and hung it on a wall of her studio. It was an illustration for a sunscreen ad in a magazine. A family having a grand old time on the beach; dad, dog, daughter, and mom applying sunscreen to the girl as she built a sand castle. She had used several photos as reference for that illustration, snapshots she had taken one summer in Xangri-Lá, where we had a beach house we eventually sold to pay off some debt. In the background, the ocean's water wasn't blue, nor were there perfect waves capped in frothy white. It was the ocean off the coast of Rio Grande do Sul, chocolate-brown, its waters choppy and turbid from high tide. A scar from a C-section ran across the mother's belly. It wasn't concealed or anything. The woman in the reference photo had one, and my mother decided to leave it in. To her surprise, the illustration had been approved and printed. It was small on the magazine page, the transgression barely noticeable and yet nonetheless there. To me, the blowup of that image on the wall telegraphed a sense of truths lingering beneath the surface, a sunny day drunk on the scent of brine, the wearisome wind always gusting along the coast.

I shuffled quietly into the studio so I wouldn't bother her, but she immediately turned her head.

"Did you find the patches?" she asked.

I said yes, that Dad was still asleep in his room, and, stepping toward her, saw her close the Facebook tab of her internet browser, revealing in its place a drawing program that she was using to illustrate some impenetrable tool. I asked her what it was. "A new kind of fruit peeler. It's all the rage at the moment." I didn't know what to say. She added that she'd be done soon and could fix us some lunch. Not wanting to bother her anymore, I went to the stacks of books scattered across the floor and on various shelves. A sudden memory buoyed me.

"Mom, do you remember how I left my copy of *Encyclopedia of Cryptozoology* here?"

It took her a moment to respond, as she finished typing something, most likely in the Facebook chat I'd interrupted.

"It's probably with the other books you left. On the white shelf, I think."

A small, Formica unit in the corner of the room, it was almost entirely subsumed by larger bookcases and stacks of books and file folders. From a distance I spotted the yellow spine of the thick hardcover volume that had been too heavy to take with me when I moved to São Paulo to do my PhD. I sat on the floor, the book cradled between my legs, flipping through it at random. "Nestor's Sea Serpent." In September 1876, in the Strait of Malacca, the crew of the SS *Nestor* spotted a creature swimming sinuously beside the ship. Reminiscent of a frog or a large gecko, its tail was over fifty meters long, its body covered in black and creamy yellow stripes. "Lake Sentani, Indonesia." At some point during the Second World War, camping with his troops on what would later become the province of Papua, in Indonesia, the anthropologist George Agogino threw a grenade into Lake Sentani, hoping to catch fish for a meal. A three-meter-long shark floated up to the surface, dead. Aside from the fact that it was found in fresh water, which was abnormal, there was nothing particularly odd about the creature. According to one hypothesis, the shark was actually a sawfish of the *Pristis microdon* species, its saw-shaped snout having been amputated by the explosion. "Diablito." Between September 2000 and February 2001, residents of Pitrufquén, a city approximately four hundred kilometers west of Buenos Aires, reported several sightings of a small, humanoid creature that they referred to as Diablito. The first few accounts were by children and not taken seriously. Before long, however, older residents also began hearing the creature's laments—"like a baby wailing"—and coming across mutilated chickens and dogs. A farmer, who claimed to have seen Diablito, described him as "a little man with the wrinkled, hairy face of a pig." Investigators noted similarities between this case and the many Chupacabra sightings across Latin America since 1995. "(Blue) Tigers." In September 1910, the Methodist missionary Harry Caldwell, a stalwart tiger hunter, came across something extraordinary in the province of Fujian in southeastern China. The specimen was described as follows, in his own words: "The animal's coat was wondrously beautiful, its base a deep grayish-blue that ranged to navy blue around its underbelly. Its stripes were well-defined and, as far as I could tell, resembled those of a standard tiger." Bernard Heuvelmans, who in the 1950s coined the term "cryptozoology," also collected accounts of blue tigers in that same region of China in 1986. And so, I bounced from entry to entry, passing the time and subduing my anxiety, which soon gave way to the sort of delight that's difficult to access after childhood. I revisited enormous owls, modern sightings of pterodactyls and other dinosaurs, legendary hominoids such as Bigfoot and Yeti, and an unending variety of sea serpents and other aquatic monsters. Most entries didn't concern such spectacular cases. Cryptozoological records are in large part composed of reports on unconfirmed species that display slight variations from known species or of already discovered species sighted in unexpected habitats. It wasn't a science, but it had a scientific bent. The *Encyclopedia of Cryptozoology* didn't feature any supernatural occurrences, UFO sightings, or anything else of the sort. It left no room for werewolves, ghosts, zombies, or large-headed aliens. The witnesses to these thousands of beings believed they had seen not otherworldly creatures but flesh-and-bone animals, children of nature no different from pigeons, horses, and human beings, animals unknown, disproportionate, and at times fantastically strange, but animals nonetheless. The volume was filled with illustrations, nearly all of them exceptionally crude. Hurried sketches by ship captains and gob-smacked naturalists, or composite sketches that suggested skepticism and scorn and were often based on myth-steeped indigenous accounts or on the testimonies of untrustworthy individuals, such as the stubbornly superstitious, or creationists out in the field seeking proof of the not-so-distant immaculate conception of our planet and its inhabitants. The *Encyclopedia* did not endorse such sources or irrational interpretations; it merely recorded them from a critical distance that seemed to imply that maybe, one day, the truth behind all those rudimentary entries might come to light. Yet it was precisely these rudimentary records and the absence of validation that had sparked my imagination at the age of ten or eleven when, for the first time, I pulled the

*Encyclopedia* from among the stacks of my mother's biology books. Those pages revealed to me a creative force that in every way surpassed any religious or mythical origin stories, a force that operated within the principles of material physics and the mechanisms of evolution, in full agreement with geology, biochemistry, and ecology. At the end of the day, an enormous, thirty-meter-long anaconda, such as the one sighted by Father Victor Heinz as he traveled by boat down the Amazon River on May 22, 1922, was improbable and as of yet unconfirmed, but not impossible, and recognizing its existence would have little effect on any extant scientific theories, even if it were then necessary to query the source of the fatty acid oxidation needed to support, calorically speaking, an animal of that size. The first-ever video footage of a giant squid in its natural habitat had been captured only recently, in July 2012, by the Japanese, thus delivering unto the profane realm of digital documentation an entire lineage of legendary sea creatures ranging from the Kraken to the Old Testament's Leviathan. Reports of dinosaurs sighted in our time were most certainly false, yet in 1938, Western scientists had discovered a coelacanth—a fish ostensibly extinct for over seventy million years—swimming in the waters off the coast of South Africa and known to its indigenous people. Even if those infinite sea serpents in folk tales and modern accounts across the world didn't really exist, they were nevertheless testaments to the fascination and horror the deep ocean and its still-mysterious inhabitants continued to inspire in the human soul. The fact was that, because of that book, I'd seen no reason to waste time as a kid on gods or ghosts when instead I could contemplate megalodons, teeny Chinese monkeys trained to prep ink for scribes, enormous infant-snatching eagles, and brutal battles between sea serpents and sperm whales, such as the one reported in 1875 by the crew of the *Pauline* off the coast of Brazil, near Capo de São Roque, a tale that eclipsed even the most fantastical passages of *Moby-Dick*, if not in philosophical density, at least in its intimation of the many fabulous creatures that nature might hold, all of which humbled and captivated me. The kingdom of unknown animals was more fascinating to me than the occult, than literature, than television.

For a couple of years after I discovered the book, whenever someone asked me what I wanted to be when I grew up, I responded—seriously and with utter conviction—that I was going to become a cryptozoologist, which to my naïve mind was a perfectly common, if not particularly popular, profession. As if this weren't enough, I had a very concrete goal: to find the white pampas deer, whose entry in the *Encyclopedia of Cryptozoology* described two sightings—one in 1940 and another in 1946—of pampas deer with fur almost entirely white. One of the eyewitnesses, a farmer from the Camaquã region, described the animal as "a full-grown pampas deer, white as a cloud, with brown spatters on its back and head, and antlers black as coal," and tried to shoot him with a rifle but missed. The other white deer had been spotted on the border of Uruguay by a group of patients from a mental asylum called Três Acácias. It might have just been a mutation of the *Ozotoceros bezoarticus* (the pampas deer)—perhaps the near-extinct *celer*, or southern, subspecies usually found in the Argentine pampas. It was certainly possible that the testimonies were false; some pampas deer really do appear whiter. But the animal in question could also have been a rare and skittish species that was seldom seen and had never been captured. This is what I believed at eleven, and a life dedicated to proving the existence of the white pampas deer seemed a good life to have ahead of me. Later, I realized that people had held back their laughter or spoken to me as if addressing a small child whenever I explained to them what the object of cryptozoological study was, and one Christmas evening, my uncle informed me that the deer in Rio Grande do Sul would soon be extinct because people in the country thought they spread hoof-and-mouth disease to their cattle and shot them on sight, and that they made good wall trophies, until finally I became embarrassed by how the grown-ups kept reacting and never mentioned it again. I spent middle school and some of high school declaring I would become an architect. It sounded like a real profession. When I graduated, I decided to try my hand at journalism, a professional track fetishized by the pseudo-cultured teens of the late nineties, the last decade when anything even resembling a market existed for that profession.

But a year later, I'd already transferred to the Biology department, which I never left. The *Encyclopedia of Cryptozoology* was at the root of my latent desire to become a scientist. That yellow-spined volume had made me see the world as a place full of concrete mysteries worth discovering and researching. As years passed, the enigmatic aura of unexplored fauna, which had made me feel as if each illustrated creature in the *Encyclopedia* had been plucked from a fairy tale or from the bestiary of a long-extinct people, began to fade away. The moment came when distinctions among new species were revealed in laboratories by means of molecular biology rather than through submarine expeditions down ocean trenches, forays into caves, or reports collected from isolated settlements. Then came the cryptozoology of gene sequencing, which occupied the water-table realm of things too small to be detected and abstract computer calculations, an intangible kingdom that paradoxically stoked our conviction that we knew the world now better than ever before, and that the only thing separating us from the still-unknown was the processing time needed to reverse the situation. Part of me couldn't reconcile this. Still fresh in my memory was a time when the unknown was still "more real" than the familiar. In my lost youth, I thought, as I sat on the floor of my mom's studio, I didn't know what to do with my urge to nose around the dark corners of our planet and universe. It had felt both exhilarating and futile, because I didn't know where to begin. I'd read issues of the magazine *Superinteres-*

*sante*, which my parents had gotten me a subscription for, and I wanted to be just like all those scientists who studied superconductors and unearthed dinosaurs, but I didn't know how to get there yet, and that felt positive, exciting. Years passed, and after a certain point, not knowing what to do with my life started feeling like a negative thing. But there was still something far worse: not wanting to do anything at all.

I shut the book over my crossed legs. Anguish seized me like a charley horse. I tried to keep it in but soon found myself sniffling. I heard my mom get up off her chair, sandals dragging along the porcelain floor, then crouch down, and I felt her hand on my shoulder. I wish I could have explained what was distressing me, but even if I had the words, I didn't have the courage. I pictured myself saying: "Mom, all that's left for this world is its destruction, and the worst thing we can do is get in its way," but I didn't even know if I really believed that, only that the notion had taken hold of me. Instead, I spoke of Dad's heart attack, how it was only just sinking in. He had nearly died. I wasn't ready for him to go. I also brought up the situation at the University of São Paulo, the risk that I might lose my grant after failing my doctoral defense because of a vindictive creep of a professor. Mom already knew about all that melodrama; we'd discussed it over several Skype sessions, one of which I spent—drunk on vodka and limoncello—elaborating on my plan to sabotage the freezers holding César's research material, to teach him that he had messed with the wrong student. She listened to me all over again and waited for me to finish before saying anything.

"Your dad's recovering well. The worst is behind us. And we've already discussed your dissertation, haven't we, honey," she said in that tone she used whenever she wanted to project her own unflappability onto other people. "Your adviser and colleagues all know the real reason you failed. Don't they? You can fix this. Your research is too valuable for them to let anything worse happen."

She mussed my hair, raised her eyebrows, and smiled with the corners of her mouth. The conversation could have ended there: she was right, I would pass on the next try, failing a defense the second time was unheard of at the Institute of Chemistry. The professor who'd replace César had nothing against me.

"Mom, do you remember Andrei? My friend, the writer."

"Yes, of course I do. Duke?"

"He died yesterday. He was killed in a robbery on Rua Ramiro."

She opened her mouth, her entire face twisting. "My God, Aurora, how awful . . ."

"They shot him in the face, all so they could steal his phone."

"That's awful. When?"

"Last night. Near Hospital de Clínicas. He lived nearby, I think."

"What a tragedy. They were always publishing pieces about him in the papers. He was doing so well for himself."

"He was."

"Did they catch the person who killed him?"

"I don't know, I don't think so."

"Are you going to the funeral? Were you in touch?"

"We hadn't spoken in a while. I haven't really kept in touch with people here since moving to São Paulo."

My mother got up and walked to the patio. I followed and found her staring at the grill. We'd held a few *Orangutan* meetings and parties there, barbecues that ran into the early morning and at times took on a psychotic or semipornographic tenor.

"I just remembered that time with the ethanol," my mother said. A plastered Andrei had once tried to light the grill with a liter bottle of ethanol, fashioning an impromptu flamethrower that roared briefly and singed a number of my mom's flowerpots and the arm hair of a kid who had to be taken to the ER. "And there was that friend of yours who was always taking his clothes off."

"Antero. Yeah, he was always doing that."

"You all still seemed like children to your dad and me. It was hard for us to come to terms with things sometimes, but eventually we got used to it."

Looking at how we were back then, it also struck me that we were just a bunch of kids. But we'd felt like grown-ups. More grown up than grown-ups. I remember vividly, in my early twenties, how I used to think of my parents as children. And now we were all more or less the same.

"Let's go see how your dad's doing," my mom said all of a sudden.

We walked into the house together and found him in his pajamas on the living room sofa, remote control in hand, watching the Buster Keaton films he so loved and had been collecting since the VHS era. I'd given him the collection on DVD for his birthday.

"You aren't supposed to laugh," my mom said.

"I've seen this film five hundred times, I don't laugh anymore," he countered.

I sat beside him, my head resting on his shoulder, my attention focused on the screen for a few minutes. In the film, Keaton played a young man with less than twenty-four hours to get married and receive his inheritance. After he was turned down by several women, his friends published a notice in the paper calling for a young bride in want of a millionaire groom. Before long, Keaton was being chased down a wide avenue by hundreds of women in wedding dresses. The pursuit spiraled into absurdity, with cranes, insane acrobatic feats between cliffs, and an avalanche that struck both our hero and his brides as they dashed down a mountainside. What I could never admit to my dad was that Buster Keaton's impassive face pulled my attention to the muscles of his spry, athletic body and that the tenacity of his characters, clumsily persisting against comically disproportionate odds, awakened in me an empathy so intense it was easily mistaken for sexual desire. As a teenager, I'd watched these tapes at home on my own, like a boy watching porn.

There was another scene, though, that unsettled me in a very different way: the closing moments of *College*, another Buster Keaton film. After an Olympic session of thwarted attempts to participate—with a modicum of dignity—in the campus's sporting life, the young student played by Keaton had finally won the affections of a lady. They married. After they left the church, a succession of three shots, fleeting as lightning, followed. The three images, one after the other, spanned no more than five seconds. First, we saw Keaton and his wife at home with their small children, absorbed in some domestic task. Then we saw the two of them, old and gray, sitting side by side in rocking chairs. Then, two gravestones. Followed by the words "The End." That ending at once terrified me and seemed to hold an urgent message: you will bend over backward and drag yourself through the mud to get what you want, and you will get it, but from that moment on, your life will be worth only three short cuts. The film had actually ended *before* those three shots, with the couple leaving the church. This was the movie's secret tragedy, its coded subtext, its nod to the absurdity of life. Of course, it had all made me love and want Buster Keaton even more. Once or twice, I had masturbated while fantasizing about his melancholy mask, his chest taut with naïve heroism.

As I sat on the sofa beside my convalescing father, I was relieved to note that my erotic relationship to Keaton's films was in the past. What held my attention then was the improbable fearlessness of his films, their suicidal recklessness shot without special effects. My dad didn't laugh at those scenes, just as he'd assured my mother he wouldn't. He watched the screen frowning and with calm focus, communing with its gentle sadness. His body smelled sour with a touch of cinnamon, and I inhaled it with a sense of transgression. My dear old man who'd almost died. I felt so close to him. Buster Keaton's on-screen energy, his malleability and unflappable demeanor were beyond our reach, but the sheer pace of the action captivating us was real, the growing momentum was real, not only real but realistic, and had long ago spilled from the big screen into our lives, which would end with three cuts so abrupt that we'd struggle to see in them a chapter of our history.

My phone vibrated in my pocket. A phone call from a number that wasn't in my list of contacts.

"Aurora?"

"Speaking. Who's this?"

"Francine. We haven't met, not in person."

But I remembered reading her name in the newspaper article.

"It's about Andrei," she said.

There's nothing pleasant about attending a funeral at a Jewish cemetery in the middle of the afternoon, legs stuck to the wet fabric of my jeans, sweat dribbling off my mustache. And things only got worse as I felt my fucking cellphone vibrate in my pocket, its ringtone resounding at a heinous volume just as, with a sinister thud, the first few shovelfuls of dirt hit the pine casket. I thought to myself that the universe really was shitting on me that day. My ringtone was the sound of those 14,400 dial-up modems that, fifteen years earlier, had lived inside everybody's PCs. Duke's friends and relatives turned their heads and looked at me with scorn, not only because I had disrupted the solemn silence but also, I supposed, because the electronic whining had dragged them back to a time when Duke had been more alive than ever, publishing his brilliant early short stories on personal websites and online literary journals.

There were no flowers in the orchard of gravestones etched with Stars of David and covered in pebbles. As I drew away from the grave and walked toward the wall that separated the cemetery from Avenida Oscar Pereira, I readjusted the yarmulke I'd been handed at the entrance, attempted to pry my cellphone from my skintight pocket and, on the way out, passed Aurora and Antero, who tried to soothe my embarrassment with sympathetic looks. I answered the call to put a stop to the ringing once and for all, only lifting the phone to my ear once I was a respectful distance from the ceremony.

"Emiliano? Can you hear me? Hello?" a familiar voice called out, deep and nasal. It was Frank, editor of Publicações Kambeba, who a few months earlier had included in his prestigious and scarcely read quarterly magazine—which was also called *Kambeba* and published essays and reportage—a long piece of mine on Chinese businessmen who were buying up large, fallow plantations in the Brazilian Midwest. Frank was a decent guy, despite his permanently grubby look and sweaty-ball stench, which he thought he masked with Lacoste cardigans and verbena cologne. He was good-natured, at least, and no doubt an excellent reader, the kind of person who could pass off years of vast, accumulated knowledge as keen intelligence.

"Hey, Frank. What's up? This isn't a good time," I said, holding the cell close to my mouth as if whispering into my own ear.

"Everything's fine. Can you not talk right now?"

"No. Call me in an hour."

"OK. Did you hear Andrei Dukelsky was murdered?"

"Yeah. I'm at the funeral."

"Huh? Speak up."

"I'm at *his* funeral."

"Oh. Great."

I remained quiet while I wondered exactly how a thing like that could be great. I had the distinct impression Frank had snorted too much coke before calling.

"I'll call you later, then," he continued. "You were good friends, weren't you?"

"We knew each other."

"Right. Great. It's a sad time. Hang in there. I'll call you later."

I hung up, switched my cell to silent, and crept stealthily back to the edge of the circle of about thirty mourners who were at the funeral. As far as I could tell, the circle consisted of family and close friends only. Duke's girlfriend, Francine, wore a straight-cut dress, long and lead-gray, her bluish veins visible in the distance, stark against her pale skin. She had an elongated jaw and prominent cheekbones, and her forehead was engulfed by long, straight bangs. If not for her full, naturally red lips, she might have looked skeletal. From certain angles, she looked like a boy. I wanted to carry on scanning her with my eyes, seeking out glimpses of masculine traits as if she were an optical illusion. Francine had reached out to Aurora, Antero, and me to inform us of the time and location of the funeral. She had emphasized the—in her words—private, almost secret nature of the ceremony. No one wanted to have to contend with the press, rivals, readers, or bootlickers. Only after taking the call did it occur to me that it was odd that she had my number, and I couldn't help wondering if at some point Duke had left her detailed instructions on how to proceed in the event of his accidental demise. Who to summon to the funeral, what to do with his manuscripts, etc. The key words were "shy," "socially awkward," "control freak," and "zero tolerance for antics." He was the kind of guy who could've written his will at thirty, meticulously picturing his own death so that he could take every possible precaution.

In attendance at the funeral—aside from the family—were Antero's wife, half a dozen faces I didn't recognize, and Nara Okamoto, Andrei's editor after his first book, a woman so highly respected in the industry that she had handily won over booksellers and secured foreign deals for all three of his novels. The other mourners, standing around the edge of the grave, were descendants of the Russian Jews who'd endowed Andrei Dukelsky with his thick eyebrows and penchant for literary prose and self-deprecation. Secular, middle-class Jews. His parents greeted us only briefly. They thanked us for attending and said Andrei had always spoken of us with fondness for the years we had spent collaborating on the e-zine. Though happy to hear this, I was saddened by the thought that we were among the few real friends he'd made in life.

Duke didn't take part in any Jewish traditions. I knew,

too, that he was a staunch atheist. To me, most of his writing could be seen to unmask millennial ideals and their hopes of transcendence, and attack the very possibility of knowledge and, above all, self-knowledge. I tried to commit this thought to memory; it would fit well in the piece that Frank had probably just called me about. Andrei's unexpected death had thrown a grenade into Brazil's drowsy literary scene—a school yard where snotty brats called each other out for their depoliticized navel-gazing. Duke didn't have time for that crap. He had just gone on publishing books that were impossible to ignore. He'd had prestige to spare, even though he was miles from landing on the best-seller list and had personally tried to smother what little fame he'd managed to secure for himself. It was about three years, as far as I could remember, since he had been on any social media or participated in any events. He had granted one of his last interviews to me, and it had been published in *Kambeba*. Frank would probably ask me to write up an obituary for the website, preferably in the form of a verbose first-person essay—all the rage just then. At first, I would say no, but then Frank would name his rate, always twice the industry standard; Publicações Kambeba and *Kambeba* were pet projects bankrolled by the fortune of a multinational pharma company that had been patenting South American botanical species for three generations. Hearing the amount he was willing to put down, I'd end up accepting, because that kind of money was all we had left. Which was what made it fucked up to be a journalist in the twenty-first century.

The funeral over, I returned my blue yarmulke with silver embroidery to the attendant at the gate, left the cemetery, lit a cigarette, and peered around me, searching for a patch of shade. The closest one was beneath the roof of a bus stop across the avenue. Way too far. Even though it was school break, the traffic was thick from the transportation strike. The scorching asphalt warped, calling to mind the crust of a river of molten lava. That heat was inhuman. Because it was linen, my shirt wasn't pasted to my body, but sweat trickled down my legs, drenching my socks. The handful of people who had come to send Duke off half-hurriedly scattered, cordially waving as they lugged themselves to their cars. I spotted a young couple standing by the gate. They hadn't even been born when I was their age. They held Andrei's books in their hands. His three bulky novels—*Bone Hill*, *Twilights of Excess*, and *Avatars*—and a rare copy of a book he'd self-published in 2002, *Two Long Stories and a Short One*. I asked if they were looking for anybody in particular. The girl, chubby in a pair of capris and a sleeveless top, wanted to know if the funeral was over. The boy, lean with a sinister Adam's apple that seemed about to burst alien-style from his neck, snapped a selfie with his cell, holding the books in the foreground, the cemetery gate behind them.

"We came for the funeral, but the family said it wasn't open to the public," the girl said woefully.

"Were there lots of people in there?" the boy asked me. "I thought there'd be at least a few out here, but I think we're the only ones." He fiddled with his cellphone some more. "Duke's trending in Porto Alegre . . ."

The girl mentioned the bus strike as a possible reason for the dearth of fans at the cemetery entrance and showed me the books she was holding, all signed by Andrei.

"We met because of his books. We went to get them signed at the book fair together. I can't believe he's gone. Think of everything he won't get to write. It's totally bizarre."

Aurora came up to me and touched my shoulder. The couple looked around, seeming unsure about what to do next, then excused themselves to walk down Avenida Oscar Pereira, hand in hand. Young readers of a young, dead author. I felt like eavesdropping on their conversation, listening to them for a few minutes, a few hours, forever.

Aurora kept her hand on my shoulder. Then, she drew closer to me, finally hugging or half-leaning on me, in a degree of physical intimacy we hadn't experienced in ages but that had in the past been routine. She seemed distracted and anxious. With my arm, I circled her body, which had grown plump with time, and on the palm of my hand felt the fine film of sweat coating her bronzed skin. Her green eyes seemed to be floating in brine. Back in our *Orangutan* days, she was always complaining that her eyes were a curse, condemning her to a lifetime of awful metaphors.

"Aurora," I murmured.

"What."

"I want to sink into your green eyes."

She didn't respond.

"Your eyes are like rare seaweed in the shallow sands of a virginal Caribbean cove."

She trembled, laughed lightly through her nose, and settled in next to me again. Ever since she had absconded to São Paulo, our contact had been sporadic, limited to the occasional Facebook comment and an annual beer or coffee. When we first met, she was a pixie-haired freshman who loved to flaunt her golden shoulders and I was the older guy who saw in her and her fresh-out-of-high-school pals a class destined for greatness or maybe even celebrity, a special crop, pioneers of a new generation that would take advantage of the internet and the country's economic stability to become more than just Mommy and Daddy's little punks, grungy suburban kids smacking their heads against their guitars, or nerds in sweat pants crusty with cum. Aurora not only had the prescience to ditch journalism while she had the chance, but also bagged a kickass prize for research she had conducted with a scientific research grant. She had devised a cutting-edge test for detecting a particular soybean pest or something like that. Even while studying and working like a maniac, fighting to carve out a space for herself in the world of science, she'd still managed to spend a few years publishing online pieces with the *Orangutan* gang—irreverent ego trips on being a young woman in Porto Alegre's underground scene as well as a column titled "So-Called Research," in which she criticized the sensationalism and inaccuracies that were part and parcel of the media's dissemination of scientific knowledge.

Antero came through the gate with his wife, Giane. He left the yarmulke on his head for a few moments, which somehow made him look more East Asian. Suddenly, he removed it and stuffed it in his pocket. Was he lifting it from the cemetery? Or did he keep a yarmulke at home for special occasions such as this one? Either hypothesis seemed plausible. Giane went to speak with Francine, and he joined us. There we were, the three remaining members of the quartet, reunited on an empty sidewalk in front of a cemetery. Duke would know what to make of that scene. Three adults compelled into silence, waiting for a complicity to blossom between them that had for years lay dormant. I lit another cigarette and felt a desperate urge to drink.

"Can I bum one?" Antero pointed at my pack of Camels. I handed him a cigarette and lit it with my lighter. "I haven't smoked in two years," he explained, "but this one's for Duke."

With the exception of the most diehard metalheads, Antero Latvala was probably the only long-haired nineties kid who'd never, at any point, sheared off his mane—that is, until earlier that year, 2014. His hair no longer fell to his ass, but instead tumbled halfway down his back, still making heads turn. Though there was something to admire in the consistency of his style, the truth was that his long, straight hair, brown with grayish streaks, had fallen over his shoulders far better at twenty than it did at thirty-something. Back then, women used to line up to blow him, or so I had witnessed once in the infamous hallway that led to the doorless bathrooms of Garagem Hermética, the site of several Orangutan parties. At the time, he was the spitting image of one of those models who strutted down runways—not the bearded lumberjacks, but the tall, squalid types who were nearly always pale with long hair and baby skin, their traits a blend of Nordic and East Asian—intimidatingly cold, exotic boys who resembled extras in sci-fi alien movies.

It was through Antero, many years ago, that I'd heard of Orangutan. I had landed on his website because of a few pieces he'd translated and published online when he was still just a kid, texts by Hakim Bey posted at a time when his work wasn't yet available in Brazil in Portuguese, even though concepts like the "Temporary Autonomous Zone" were all the rage with young journalists and Communications majors. Antero's site also included a link to the homepage of the email e-zine he'd started with Duke during a state college strike that had left them twiddling their thumbs. It had all started, really, with the mile-long emails Antero would send to his classmates, filled with pornographic stories, poems in free verse peppered with links that led down bizarre internet rabbit holes, reviews of films and CDs, and myriad artistic manifestos penned under the influence of marijuana, LSD, downtime, and sui generis interpretations of post-Structuralist thinkers. His classmates started replying with their own contributions, and eventually it occurred to Duke to transform these long, spontaneous missives into a text-only publication that would be distributed bi-weekly via email. Aurora capped the trio of columnists. After contributing a few of my own texts, I approached them and joined the permanent team. At our most popular, we had thousands of readers, dozens of whom regularly sent in pieces. Though it lasted no more than two years, it had changed our lives. Like any temporary autonomous zone, *Orangutan* was a hiccup, a project fated to fail that nonetheless infused everyone involved with a tremendous energy. It'd been a long time since I had experienced that vitality in what I did or in the people I worked with.

The Antero majestically dragging on that cigarette by the cemetery was a different sort of creature to the young man of bygone days, the heartthrob son of Finnish immigrants who'd cooked up poetic acts of terrorism as part of a utopian project whose goal was to wrest Porto Alegre from its provincial coma. I knew that for some years now he'd been heading his own "illustrious" advertising agency, which took up two whole floors of a building in Moinhos de Vento. Legions of viral videos, memes, and controversial commercials that popped up all over the media and carried his secret signature in their slogans. He'd put on weight, or maybe it was more accurate to say that he had filled out or puffed up, like an alcoholic. At twenty, Antero had been one of those naturally lean kids with a brisk metabolism. He'd drink condensed milk straight from the can on doctor's orders, anytime, anywhere, with scarcely veiled swagger, and even then didn't gain weight. The spell had dried up. We were standing before the physical wreckage of a former sex symbol.

Giane said goodbye to Francine and came to meet us. An imposing woman, she was the epitome of Serra Gaúcha beauty, a bona fide Grape Festival princess raised on a diet of pasta and polenta, with shockingly blond hair and large, blue Italian eyes. Her sweat had blurred her mascara. Of all of us, she was the person least vulnerable to the sad circumstances that had brought us together, and her attitude was as respectful as it was blasé. She hadn't been close to the deceased in any way, though this didn't strike me as reason enough to justify her rarefied air. I would have bet that she'd lost many loved ones. After throwing each of us equal doses of compassionate looks, she rested her hand on Antero's shoulder. I noticed him shield his cigarette with his body, which was no more than a considerate gesture, seeing as his smoke left a tar miasma in the stuffy air.

"Hon . . . Are you staying with them?" Giane asked.

Antero looked at me. At Aurora.

"Yeah. Let's go get a beer in the Cidade Baixa. A quickie."

We hadn't made any plans, and yet Antero's impetuous decision suddenly took hold of us and became irrevocable.

"We haven't seen each other in ages," Antero added, and Giane broke into a warm smile.

"Of course. Go, go. I'll pick Miguel up from Mom's. We'll see each other later. Do you have a ride?"

"I've got my dad's car," Aurora said.

Giane kissed Antero, said goodbye, and walked down the sidewalk along Avenida Oscar Pereira toward the parking lot, heels clacking off the basalt slabs.

"How old is he?" Aurora asked.

"Two," Antero responded, showing us the boy on his iPhone homescreen, playing on a floor that resembled a colorful foam puzzle designed to keep rug rats from breaking. Antero's Finnish genes were stamped all over the boy's face. His eyes were slanted, and he had a chin like a Ping-Pong ball.

"Where are we going? I'll meet you there. I have to deal with something first," I found myself saying. Aurora insisted on giving me a ride wherever I needed to go, recalling that the city was short on buses, but I was unrelenting. "I'll meet you all soon. I won't be a minute."

Antero's eyes suddenly glimmered. "You know where we should go? Sabor Um. For the good old days."

They went to Aurora's car, which was parked beside that same stretch of sidewalk, and I walked at a clip down Avenida Oscar Pereira, skirting the cemetery. I veered into the streets of Medianeira, passing dilapidated walls still plastered with ads for the last election's congressional candidates, children fooling around during summer break, and teenagers smoking weed and maneuvering skateboards around an abandoned playground, tufts of grass bristling through the cracks in the cement.

I turned corners at random as if searching for the source of the soft scent of rot that had infested the city ever since the first heat wave had hit. On some lost block in the heart of Azenha, I came across an empty lot with a wall of half-crumbling bricks and walked in. Amid the tall grass were remnants of construction material, disintegrating clothing, plastic bags tangled in the boughs of bushes, and a bunch of used condoms, dry and creased like snakeskin. At the back of the lot, I spied a whitish object. An old washing machine, on the small side. I kicked it with all my strength. The vegetation kept the rusted cube from going very far. I kept kicking and pummeling the lid with clenched fists and then lifted the machine above my head and hurled it against the wall of the house next door. I kicked it some more, until I was spent.

I didn't wait to catch my breath before lighting a cigarette. I saw a little blood on my hands, but they were just skinned. I felt dizzy, but my body remained firm, both feet planted on the ground. I flexed my arm and decided that it still had some punch in it. Those bones and tendons were under my control, full of power. I tensed my abdomen. Let a jab, a battering ram, a fucking train come at me; I was ready. I exited the lot and glanced around me to see if I had caught the attention of any neighbors, but the cobblestoned street was still as quiet as I had found it.

I arrived at Sabor Um about half an hour later, stinking to high hell, my hair slick with sweat. After burning off a fair amount of energy by bashing the washing machine and charging down fifteen blocks, all while smoking, I was forced to accept the hard truth of the matter. I was a forty-two-year-old schlub. A trash bag with arms and legs. Aurora and Antero were sitting at a small metal table, the only one occupied in that empty bar, speaking animatedly. It was almost eight p.m., but the pale light tinted the gray flagstones yellow. With daylight savings, sunset was still only a distant promise.

"There's blood on your shirt," Aurora said.

I sat wordlessly, my face set in its best "don't ask" expression.

"It isn't the same," Antero said, pointing with his chin at the enormous half-eaten meat pastel, the deep-fried dough gleaming.

"I'm sure the pastels are still the same," Aurora said with good-natured weariness. "It's just that Antero only eats at fine restaurants these days. He asked, no joke, if I've been to D.O.M. in São Paulo. What kind of ridiculous question is that? I live off boiled peas, pasta, and canned tuna, you bastard."

I ordered a cold bottle of Serramalte beer, topped up our three glasses, and toasted to Andrei. We spent a few minutes discussing the crime and the investigation. They hadn't found the killer, nor would they, we thought. The police solved fewer than 10 percent of murder cases across the state. The latest online was that they were collecting footage from the cameras in the neighboring buildings, searching for leads.

"It's easier to go to prison for filming cops shooting rubber bullets at people than for stabbing someone," I said. "To this day, there are kids in prison for carrying vinegar in their backpacks at protests last year."

Antero looked at me as if I had just stuck him up with a carving knife.

"What?" I pushed, confused by his reaction.

"You covered the June protests, right?" he asked, bumming another Camel. What a little shit, I thought. Didn't he have money enough to buy his own? I said I had reported on a few protests here in Porto Alegre for *Válvula*, an alternative journalism site. He nodded and took a drag from his cigarette as I waited in vain for him to draw the discussion out. But it was Aurora who broke the silence.

"Safety isn't the only issue," she snarled. "It's this strike keeping buses off the streets, the heat making everybody crazy, the water shortages, blackouts, and all those people living on the streets like animals. I can't bring myself to believe things will ever get better. Any old fool knows what's wrong and what could be done to fix it, but what could be done won't be done, and it's impossible to believe it'll ever get done. I'm becoming one of those people who seriously buys into the end of the world. I always thought they were so ridiculous."

"Things end up falling into place," Antero said, just as I opened my mouth in protest. "Humankind adapts. Ever since there's been language, we've believed in the apocalypse. Every century, in every culture. Human beings create these sorts of myths precisely because the end of the world is something that systematically *doesn't happen.* Remember Y2K?"

Aurora started shaking her head. But, in a way, I thought he was right.

"I don't know," she continued, sounding blue. "What happened to Duke has left me feeling like it's already ended."

"What's ended?"

"Everything! Have you not walked down the street lately? Porto Alegre is like a chicken with its head cut off, scrambling around the backyard in its last few moments of life. In São Paulo they're saying the city's going to run out of water. I try to take everything I read about climate change, radiation, and mass extinction with a grain of salt. But yesterday felt like a slap to the face."

I cut her off a bit brusquely, noting that a good friend of ours had just died in a stupid, random way because of the wretchedness that had shadowed humanity since its inception, but that there was nothing new or unusual about it. It had nothing to do with global warming or the end of the world. Only one world had ended: Andrei's. He alone had known that world. And he'd strived to share it in the only way he could, with literature, in a struggle that had consumed him to the point of near social autism. The moral of the story in all this was the prevalence of what made us human, including our fears of death and the apocalypse. It was the dissemination and propagation of these and all our other feelings and values—no matter how fucked we or the world were—toward that idyllic unity in which life was erased only to then be reconciled; it was our access to other lives, a surrender that allowed us to dissolve *in life* rather than *in death*; death, which would arrive sooner or later anyway, but shouldn't at the age of thirty-six with a gunshot to the head over a goddamned cellphone. I didn't express myself in exactly those words, but confused, shaken, and drunk as I already was, the phrases I spewed onto the table of that bar that had once been so special to us ran vaguely along those lines. Both Aurora and Antero put up with my raving. It wasn't the first time they had seen me riled up. With other people, in similar situations, I would feel like a caged animal that'd be denied food unless it calmed down. With them, and with Duke, it was different. It was like they were in the cage with me, responding instead of just reacting to me on the other side of the bars. Near me. On the inside.

We moved from the subject of civilization's imminent demise to reminiscing about our first few years in Duke's company: the first stories he'd published online, always anxious for our thoughts, trying to affect humility in the face of our critiques; later, the books he'd self-published with public funding and money from his own pocket; his rare and sudden bursts of camaraderie and surrender to his friends' physical affection; his early charisma, which had diminished as his books gained readers and respect, finally giving way to a manner at once impatient and impenetrable. In a way, the Duke who sat beside us at the table was the Duke from 1999—when they were eighteen years old and I was twenty-seven—the year we had lived our lives with an intensity that would forever remain unrivaled.

Night fell, finally, and with it we turned to discussing our lives. Antero tried to explain the affairs of his company, which traded in communications and trends—or was it publicity and marketing, or market-oriented gamification and ethnography? In any case, it was some sort of large-scale hoax. In the past few years, though, he had managed to secure clients such as Ambev, Volkswagen, Sony, and Unilever. He traveled to São Paulo every two weeks and abroad at least once a month. Although I knew that he had become some sort of adman, until that day in Sabor Um, I hadn't had a clue of his company's magnitude. He must have been a millionaire. I pictured him hollering, "Surgical strike!"—or any one of those antithetical expressions-turned-buzzwords that echoed Paul Virilio—invoking the contradictions of post-modernity in a hipster-style office filled with self-diagnosed creatives enjoining the team to concoct new formulas for selling cars to a generation that was increasingly disinterested in them. There was a brutal irony to his trajectory, one he seemed to be fully aware of. In the early 2000s, Antero had been one of the most provocative figures of Porto Alegre's cultural scene. He had organized events and art exhibits in the galleries and abandoned buildings on the working-class fringes of town, such as Galeria Coruja de Minerva in Medianeira and in public squares around Restinga. He had recited his impenetrable texts at soirées composed of at most half a dozen people. For years after *Orangutan*'s end, he'd kept a blog on which he habitually published endless posts on the society of spectacle, rhizomes, and simulacra. Any old layabout could have dropped those sorts of concepts into their conversations or articles in an attempt to appear clever in the small cosmos of our Humanities department. But Antero in fact read Debord, Deleuze and Guattari, Baudrillard, Benjamin, and the other thinkers whom the less demoralized professors still sought to teach their Social Communications students. He had also read evolutionary psychology, Chinese and ancient Greek philosophy, Freud, Foucault. He'd gone through a different phase every two to three months: moral animal, cyborg, Zen, androgyne, anarchist. Each accompanied by a new, corresponding look, like the Edu K of academic syllabi. His hair remained long, but its color changed with his clothing, accessories, and gestures. He read more than anyone, even more than Duke, but the end result of his voracity was an incoherent potpourri of thoughts and quotations fired off for maximum seductive effect, without necessarily meaning anything in the context of a particular debate or situation. His daily spiel was a vast, unfinished canvas onto which he copied and pasted ideas without much criteria or sense of how it went together. Antero's mind was then, before the turn of the century, a sampling of what thought would become in the age of Google and Wikipedia. If in those days it had a touch of the avant-garde—inspiring a mixture of fascination and bewilderment in those who read his online manifestos or listened to his torrents of catchphrases—it now served mostly to lend cultural cachet to the brands, products, and services of his clientele. He operated like a marketing guru, that is, like a buffoon. To my eyes, his existence was like an absurdist skit with no programmed end, unable to tell life from the stage. Had it a purpose, it might have been genius. Maybe it was. No one could know for sure.

It was impossible not to pick up on the lascivious, quasi-maniacal looks that Antero kept throwing Aurora throughout the night. Looks that didn't even desist when she told us, over our eighth bottle of Serramalte, about her father's near-death and the encroaching threats to her career. A vindictive professor had sabotaged her doctoral defense at the University of São Paulo. Any further hitches and she might lose her grant. A soft electrical current seemed to straighten her spine and brighten her eyes when she described the ins and outs of her research, which sought to better understand the circadian rhythm of sugarcane. Hers was an ambitious project with varied implications, above all the possibility of achieving game-changing results for the world of agrobusiness.

"Sugarcane has this internal oscillator," she explained with gestures and slurred words, wagging her index finger like a metronome, "through which environmental stimuli enter, setting off its circadian clock and generating rhythms. I'm researching how sugarcane processes these signals, informing the cells that it's day or night, in order to calibrate its growth, photosynthesis, etc."

I remember thinking that few people on Earth deserved to be compensated for their lives' endeavors as much as she did. I felt the bracing desire that she do well in everything and have cause to be happy in the coming years. She looked lovely with her hair up in a bun and her neck moist with sweat. There was a time many years ago when I'd mistaken the boundless affection Aurora awakened in me for sexual desire, for the shadow or threat of it, all of which had left me feeling afflicted. Antero mentioned something about a physics book he had read by an author who denied the existence of the flow of time, and they both threw themselves into an impenetrable discussion. I was well-acquainted with the flow of time and not particularly interested in discussing whether it existed or the ways in which it fucked me on a molecular level. I got up and announced that I was going to the restroom to study the flow of my urine.

At the table beside the bar's entrance, an elderly white-haired man, fleshy as a walrus, with a tracheal tube lodged in his saggy neck, sat whispering hoarsely to the bar owner, who, with a rag doused in rubbing alcohol, wiped down the stainless steel bar on which the lunch buffet was served. The fatty scent of food lingered in the hot air. The restroom brought back pleasant memories. I'd fucked there twice, once doubled over that urinal. Amazing, I thought, how in the past people would fornicate in bar bathrooms across Porto Alegre. Men and women stopping for a quickie in the stalls of Bambu's, Garagem, or Dr. Jekyll in much the way people these days step onto the street to smoke cigarettes. A little mirror with a plastic, orange-colored frame had once hung on that wall. It was gone. As I washed my hands with green soap from one of the rotating glass soap dispensers, my cellphone began ringing. It was Frank, wanting to know if I could talk. I said yes and took a seat on the toilet. I tried to mask my inebriation. He asked about the funeral, if there had been any press, if I had spoken to the family. Then he said that he had a proposition for me. He wanted me to write about Duke. Just as I'd predicted.

"Is it for the website?" I asked, somewhat impatient, already thinking he wouldn't want to pay me. "When's the deadline? What's the word count?"

The sound of barking dogs barreled down the line, and Frank yelped at them to shut up. They all obeyed, except for one that kept growling. Frank had a fat, blind Weimaraner and a bunch of other small dogs that featured daily on his Instagram.

"Emiliano, pay attention. Are you drunk? I said biography, an actual biography. A book."

Only then did it click. I knew at once that it was an awful idea and that I was fucked, because I'd end up accepting, and that would be the end of me.

"Andrei was thirty-six, Frank. He was a healthy, balding Jewish kid with a shitload of talent, sure, but he wasn't exactly what anyone would call a good subject. He wasn't around long enough to merit a biography."

"I disagree," Frank said again and again over what I was saying. "Andrei was a mystery, Emiliano, a fascinating figure who's become even more fascinating because he's died young, and tragically. And there are two reasons why I'm convinced he's a good subject. First, that internet zine thing you were all doing in the nineties, *Orangutan*. The generation that caught the beginning of the internet revolution, pre–political correctness and the professionalization of the net. The generation that created tools and established precedents for the kids who came later, and that then, when the internet was ransacked and disfigured by big corporations, sort of quietly withdrew."

"Frank, look . . ." I tried to interrupt, but it was pointless.

"The second reason is that all his discretion and reclusiveness, the seemingly normal little life he tried to cultivate, they just don't mesh with what he wrote. There's a kind of deception going on there. Look at his characters. Andrei wrote like a fifty-year-old man living several lives at once. There's something missing in this picture, not just a gap, but an entire untold story—about his personal life and how he worked. I'm sure of it."

"It's obvious he did research, but—"

"Maybe it was all research and maybe his life was more complex than what he had to show for it. It doesn't matter. Even if it was all research, that's a story in itself, how he conducted his research. C'mon, it'd make a hell of a book."

"Won't a magazine article do?"

"Did you know that *Bone Hill* has sold sixty thousand copies, not counting government sales? Almost every young author today copycats that book. Next year, there'll be a film adaptation of *Avatars* by a young director who won a prize at Sundance. Everything's going to be adapted to film. And I don't think you've paid close enough attention to what's going on online. The tributes, the photos people kept of him, videos of people reading, crying. And he's long been studied in academic circles. You're not following these things. It's very special. Trust me. It's a snowball that just won't stop rolling, not anytime soon. He died just as he was on the verge of *blowing up*. That's why I think it has to be a book. Not an article. It'll rain articles. I want a book."

"All right, Frank, but the thing is I'm not sure I'm comfortable writing it."

"You were close friends, I know. But that's exactly why I think you're the guy for the project, besides the quality of your writing, of course. It's got to be someone who sort of already knows where to look."

And then he spoke of the advance he could offer as well as money for research and travel expenses. Drunk as I was, the calculation was still pretty straightforward. Frank was offering me more money than I could make in a semester of writing pieces for websites, newspapers, and magazines. He would probably give me more if I asked for it. A fortune from patenting plants that the indigenous people of South America had known and used for millennia.

"The only thing is, the turnaround has got to be fast," Frank added. "So that it sells, so that we can ride the coattails of his death and, I know, I know it's depressing things work this way, but they do, the book needs to be done in five, six, seven months tops. I'll need a first draft by then so we can work on it together some more."

It sounded like Frank had tired of speaking, and I was tired of listening. I suspected that he had become enamored of Duke. Or that he knew something I didn't. Or maybe Frank was just right about the posthumous phenomenon rounding the corner. We remained quiet for a moment, Frank breathing down the line, me sitting on that toilet that stank of Cheetos, someone outside forcing the knob repeatedly to let me know it was time to get out. The bar must have been filling up out there.

"I'm going to have to think about it, Frank."

I hung up, flushed, jostled the little bearded fellow awaiting his turn so that he'd know who was boss, and walked back to the table. I decided not to tell Aurora and Antero. The mere fact that I had passively submitted to that conversation while Duke's body was still warm filled me with guilt. I struggled to understand the grain of the emotion Frank's proposition had moved in me. Revealing Duke's story meant revealing certain parts of myself I was probably unwilling to sift through and divulge. The bar was, in fact, fuller. Two more tables had been occupied by undernourished college kids. I informed my two old friends that I'd have one more drink and then head home, that work had called and I needed to write a few lines for the following morning. They nodded without paying me much mind. Things had progressed. Their body language was hard to miss. Aurora's shoulders were trained at Antero like harpoons, accenting the lustrous concavity of her clavicles, her neck exposed as if to a bite. He had the circumspect look of someone whose mind was already one step ahead, machinating the events that would unfold far from that table. It was curious to say the least. For years, Aurora had snubbed Antero's advances. Though they had always gotten along well as friends, his physical presence had provoked in her an almost elemental repulsion. Aurora was more interested than most in what Antero had to say, which was likely the source of their chemistry. We kissed and hugged. I walked out of the bar convinced that they'd leave that place to screw like rabbits in some vile motel they had visited with other bodies in their youth, and which would inspire in them a nostalgia for a time when they had been too young to bother with hygiene, moral hangovers, or getting up early the next day. I didn't envy them.

At home, the first thing I did was turn on the noisy AC unit in the living room, then take a shower under the hot water coming from the cold-water pipes. There was no cold water in the taps of Porto Alegre those days. Even Lago Guaíba ran warm. You had to visit the fridge or travel seaside for any respite. I opened my laptop, scanned my mp3 folders. I put Elliott Smith on shuffle and started clicking through old photos from the *Orangutan* days. They were tiny, no larger than three hundred pixels across, either shot with first-generation digital cameras or scanned from enlarged negatives that had been sized to fit on the internet of the time—dial-up.

Duke was all but a baby in those pictures. Even the premature widow's peak that'd made an appearance in his twenties was missing. A weird pompadour topped his head, the handiwork of a talentless barber he'd insisted on frequenting. Duke was as lanky as the rest of us. Aurora and Antero looked even younger than he did, bona fide high-school youths. Several of the photos had been snapped by the pool at barbecues held at Aurora's parents' house. Antics featuring inflatable gators and jugs overflowing with caipirinhas. Baby-faced boys playing at snuff. Girls oozing natural collagen and smoking crooked cigarettes. Friends and zine contributors posing together or doing sexy little dances in bathing suits beneath streams of water from the hose or fencing with barbecue skewers still decked in chicken hearts and hunks of rib meat. Somebody hungover napping on the sofa, a book by Hilda Hilst splayed on their belly. And then there were the shots snapped at bars, clubs, or musical and literary soirées. I was there, in some of them, a tall, bearded man with facial acne and greasy hair who resembled the leader of a murderous sect or, worse yet, one of those young-at-heart dads who wants to chill with his kid's friends. All in all, there weren't very many, only about sixty or seventy photos spanning a period of about four years. From a hyper-documentary perspective—as had become the norm in recent years—they were touching in their documentary concision. I stumbled on something unexpected besides the photos. In the same folder, a lone video file titled "myvideo.mp4." Much like any digital film from the nineties, it was a real relic; few had survived the obsolescence of physical media.

I was one of tens or hundreds of people who had watched that film in the months the file was passed from hand to hand on a CD-ROM. It was two minutes and two seconds long. I hit play. A long-haired boy with an adolescent physique entered the scene wearing only a white shirt whose sleeves, roughly cut with scissors, exposed lean, muscular shoulders. His back seemed purposefully rounded, forming a hump that contrasted grotesquely with his spry, limber figure. He was barefoot, his legs wide open, knees bent and forearms resting on his thighs, advancing crablike to the center of that small, white-walled room. The first time I watched that video, I thought it showed a drunk teenager posing like a sumo wrestler to entertain his equally dimwitted friends, though his bare, bony ass and scrotum swinging mere inches from the floor immediately belied this first interpretation, hinting at something far stranger. The video's resolution, almost certainly shot with one of those MiniDV camcorders popular at the time, had been reduced to 320 by 240. The conversion from cassette to digital had been imperfect, and the image had been chewed up by the brutal video compression of the pre-broadband days, such that the various components in the scene struggled to become clearly defined. Viewed years later, the video seemed like it had been shot with a security or spy camera, a mosaic of ochre and greenish pixels obtained via fraudulent means. The boy's form came into focus, no longer obstructing the scene and revealing a two-colored parquet. Naked, equally adolescent girls emerged sprawled across the entire floor, all of them belly-up, their arms stretched out in the shape of a cross and their hair splayed behind them. The whites of their wide-open eyes popped in an incongruent glimmer that appeared moist in that low-resolution video, at first view reminiscent of something vaguely sexual and now, nearly fifteen years later, on that night heading into dawn, evoked mollusks and mother-of-pearl. The mouths of some were half-open in the manner of corpses or, perhaps more accurately, of models posing in a photography studio for one of those fashion shoots whose necrophiliac approach was only thinly disguised. A few seconds later, you could make out a total of three girls. His back still to the camera, the boy advanced farther, placing his feet at the shoulders of one of the girls, a short-haired brunette with a black handkerchief, or some sort of collar, fastened around her neck, and lowered his haunches slowly, sitting on her face. The lighting had been meticulously rigged. A pedestal mount with a light point was visible in the left corner of the screen. Offscreen, a light source placed close to the ground cast long shadows of the half-silhouetted girls on the floor, dressing their contours in a whitish glow. It occurred to me that, aside from the eroticism in the foreground, the setting sort of resembled a sci-fi landscape, as if the rising sun were shining light onto creatures lying on the surface of an inhospitable planet monitored by a robot's lo-fi camera. The boy moved his hips back and forth, his ass grinding on the face of one of the girls, who responded with a slight flex of her legs. You could see, from the way his elbow moved, that he held his cock in his left hand, slowly masturbating. With his free right hand, he grabbed the black collar around the girl's neck, using it as a handle to keep his balance and, at the same time, to pull her head between his legs. Any sneaking suspicion that the video might be a clip from a commercial pornographic production could be ruled out at that point, not only because of the dark aesthetic approach to that mise-en-scène but also because of the absence of a characteristic trait of directed porn. The participants were having fun. On top of this, a naïve levity set the video apart from other similar cultural artifacts, such as *2 Girls 1 Cup*, which would become pop phenomena in later years. In the following seconds, for example, the boy allowed the short-haired brunette a moment to breathe then connected his buttocks again to her face and shimmied as if he were dancing lambada, making one of the girls next to him, a redhead, grin. Had the film been shot in 2014, it would no doubt have joined the flux of amateur videos uploaded by the second to the internet. It would have been chewed up, digested, and defecated throughout the web, a cesspool of digital content. But back then, when video streaming was still a novelty of limited efficacy, those images exuded an air of the avant-garde while simultaneously ragging on the egotism of sexual fetish videos with a detachment at once jocular, juvenile, spoiled, and obscene, and yet possessed of intent. You had to watch the film several times before you could commit to memory what was going on. It wasn't scandalous. Just unexpected. After sitting on the first girl's face, the boy repeated this stunt with the other two. The second girl's jaw—her feet angled at the camera—jutted frighteningly and her nostrils quivered as he sat down and began his toing and froing. For the first time, you could glimpse his erect cock, smooth and uniform like a thing just-birthed by Mother Nature, rooted in its hairy pubis. He clutched his cock with his hand, squeezing it at regular intervals as if milking himself. He never looked directly at the camera, though his naked face and long, straight, grayish hair tumbled down his shoulders. He was as beautiful as a teenage hero in a Japanese anime, with narrow eyes that appeared exotic beside his Western features, tubular nose, and square jaw. He could've stepped right out of a new Gus Van Sant film. His sinewy abdomen rippled like a dancer's. He raised his haunches a few centimeters so the girl could breathe, and she raised her head, her lips soft, the tip of her tongue poking out, as if she wanted to continue sipping from some vital source, her eyes closed and face glistening with saliva, chest rising and falling. Watching that video years later, I couldn't say whether it repulsed or excited me. It was neither one nor the other. It was all so uncanny that the images took on an odd, metaphysical aura; they relied on nothing, owed nothing, and had the autonomy of things both unreal and quasi-real, like a tesseract or Bigfoot. There was barely a sound beyond the music playing on offstage speakers. A song from Low's first album, a sleepy tune with succinct lyrics. *"I'm sorry but I can't hold on. It works much better if I let it drag me around."* It had been one of my favorite albums, and I'd come to it, precisely, through that video. A friend of mine had managed to identify the song and had lent me the imported CD he'd ordered from a record store on Rua Marechal Floriano. Then, at some point in 1999, I had downloaded the tracks as mp3s on Soulseek, via dial-up connection, and burned a CD I played over and over until it was worn out. The song added an extra layer of irony to the video because it seemed more suitable as a lullaby for the existentialist contemplations of a young European director trying to emulate Wim Wenders, rather than the anilingual contra dance of a Gen Y buck and three nymphets. It was easy enough to switch off the volume in my head and picture the film's soundtrack as a classic, kick-ass tune from the nineties, like Portishead's trip-hop tracks or the final cathartic minutes of Smashing Pumpkins' "Starla," the kind of racket that set you moshing in those little infernos of Porto Alegre during the last gasps of the millennium. The soundtrack was, in other words, the only seemingly arbitrary aspect of the video's aesthetic. It was as if the song had simply been playing when they'd decided to press record on the handycam. The boy crab-stepped to the third girl, the redhead, who was lying to the left of the frame, most of her out of view. Only her head of wavy, copper-colored hair, petite breasts, and a pair of prominent ribs were in sight. The boy's posture made me think of something else, the trial scene in Pink Floyd's *The Wall*, when the judge morphs into a gigantic bipedal butt. The redhead ran her tongue from the boy's testes to the bone that jutted from his sacrum, just above his buttocks, back and forth. She spat upward and let the saliva run back down her unfurled tongue. The redhead was the one trying the hardest to pull off these so-called sordid stunts. His body's vitality, composed entirely of tendons, was visible even in that mosaic of pixels. Another few seconds passed, and then, in a swift motion, the redhead leapt out from under the guy's legs and gripped him forcefully by the chest, knocking him off balance and onto the floor. She pounced with commendable power and flexibility, like a serpent striking, but without an ounce of aggression. On the contrary, hers was an amorous leap that seemed to surge from a dammed tenderness that burst ahead of schedule. The two of them hugged and laughed in the middle of the room. Their straight, long hair mixed into a single silky fabric that covered them down to their elbows. Slits in that gleaming curtain opened and closed, revealing ears, lips, and shoulders. I felt the urge to hug them, too, to inhale the scent of their hair. In the final moments, the two other girls looked at each other, as if pressed to improvise, and after a moment's hesitation, also nestled into each other, though without the same drive, their legs crisscrossing slowly. Cigarettes were lit in bursts of yellow light. Something strange was taking place. For the first time, the camera started moving, shaking and ascending, as if it had come loose from its tripod and was slowly rotating backward. Though expecting to see the face of the person behind the camera, what emerged instead after the 180-degree rotation was a wall bearing an inscription. Perhaps the camera operator had shifted his own body so as not to appear in the image. Yet it had all transpired so smoothly, and the expectation of being met with a human face had seemed so inevitable, that its absence left a phantasmagoric effect. In it, we were faced with a thing inhuman. The lens focused slowly or was slowly focused on the inscription, and after a few moments we could read, in black marker over the white wall, "The worst form of vanity is to expect recognition for our sacrifices." The video ended, at its most predictable moment.

I rearranged myself on the sofa and lit a cigarette. A garbage collector was tearing apart some discarded object on the sidewalk in front of the building. A sink or a toilet bowl. The sound of shattering drowned out his bickering with the outraged neighbors. Those photos and that video were traces of a past that flooded my mind in those early-morning hours. As if the mere sight of a hunk of volcanic rock could awaken a volcano. The man who'd conceived of the video and starred in it was Antero Latvala. He was eighteen when he had made it, moments before becoming a minor celebrity in the underground scene. The redhead hugging him at the end was his girlfriend of the time, Priscila, who later went on to become one of *Orangutan*'s most active contributors, though she was never on the permanent team. I couldn't remember who the other two were. Probably a couple of wild girls he'd picked up at some rave in the now-extinct Neo nightclub or at a college party. And the apartment where the video had been shot was the kitchenette rental Duke had lived in at the time. He was the one handling the camcorder and who had written that phrase on the wall. Those words found their way onto the epigraph of his first published novel, attributed to a fictitious Chinese sage. Some readers recognized it as a reference to a cult video from the dawn of the internet, but despite the fact that this information could be found on his Wikipedia page, almost no one knew that Andrei Dukelsky had been the one behind that camera or that the slogan was his.

The sound of the intercom pierced my ears, a single protracted buzz followed by a short one, Manfredo's trademark. I didn't move at first, savoring the foolish delusion that he might think I wasn't home, but the light from the living room table lamp, which sat beside the window of my second-floor apartment, gave me away. I waited for it to ring a second time, and it did, as expected, even longer than the first. I peeked through the window. He had already locked his fixie to the building's grille fence, a sign that he not only expected but was certain he'd be let up. I closed my laptop and went to the kitchen to answer the intercom, grabbing a KitKat from the fridge while I was at it.

"Hello."

"Hi, Emiliano. What's up?"

"Nothing."

"I know I shouldn't be coming around, but I wanted to see if I could come up to talk."

I unwrapped the KitKat bar.

"I thought it was clear we shouldn't for a while."

"C'mon, man."

The KitKat instantly melted in my hands. I shoved the entire thing in my mouth.

"What're you eating?"

"A KitKat. Look, Manfredo, I can't talk right now. I want to be alone, I've had a rough day, and I've got things I want to think about. We can talk tomorrow. We can grab lunch, if you want."

"Lunch? I'm downstairs, Êmi. I slept over at your place for weeks, and now suddenly I'm not welcome anymore? I guess stepping all over people comes naturally to you."

The gateway to drama was creaking and seemed ready to swing wide open. One of the drawbacks of being a gay man was all this teetering back and forth between fuckfests and desperate romantic attachment, with nothing in between. You were either screwing three guys in the same night without exchanging more than a dozen words or falling prey to commitments marked by neediness and obsession and which, at the slightest sign of trepidation, turned into recurring debates on character and emotions. I had until then found only solitude and anguish between those two poles, along with the certainty that real affection was unviable, so you might as well not even try. I was sick of that bullshit. Manfredo was the youngest, most sensitive guy I had ever tried to become involved with, and clearly it had gone wrong. A militant advocate of bike lanes and the preservation of our city's public spaces, Manfredo worked in postproduction and dabbled in 3-D animation. Except, ever since I had known him, he had only worked for free. He lived off a monthly stipend from his dad, though he denied it. He didn't excite me much sexually, either. I liked his long beard and robust body, but his skin was soft, and his prudishness got on my nerves. Manfredo was vegan and had two cats. He didn't think that it was inconsistent to be vegan and castrate his cats, but I did. Killing to eat was immoral, and castrating a domestic animal, in his egotistical, anthropocentric view, was humanitarian. What the cat thought of that, if it was partial to fucking boundlessly, scuffling with other cats, and running away—the cat's inner life—didn't matter to him. He accused me of being ignorant about companion species. This was the topic that compelled me to send him out to pasture. I recognized, after unilaterally ending our weeks-long relationship, that I had been seduced by his youth, and nothing else. A foolish temptation, as if he could have palliated the feeling I'd had since turning forty that I was already in the process of decomposing. In that moment, though, I would rather have been a carcass than let him up.

After pushing back several more times, I heard Manfredo unlock his bike from the fence and leave behind, in that sweltering night, only the vibrations of his sorrow. I opened another pack of Camels and a can of beer and watched the video another half-dozen times, unmoved by the images yet sensitive to Duke's presence behind the camera—intensely engaged without engaging, which is how he always engaged in things. That video was the reason I had gone up to Antero at a party in Ocidente in early 1999, to compliment him on what was, in effect, the first viral video produced on *gaúcho* soil. As he went on—without a scrap of modesty—about how his video's aesthetics foreshadowed a future in which the web and virtual reality would foster a vicarious and detached sexuality, a friend of his had approached us and was soon introduced to me as "Duke, our zine's only real writer." A boy with a seasoned face that begged for muttonchops, he wore a white shirt under a brown velvet blazer that didn't jibe with all the Smiths T-shirts, flannel jackets, and leather vests around us. We met at one of the parties that used to be held every Friday at Ocidente, whose patrons were mostly gay men but also a bunch of straight kids who liked rocking out to Madonna, Duran Duran, and the Village People with a touch of subversion but no real risk. People like the *Orangutan* gang, whom I'd been following with great interest but had never met in person. Antero excused himself to go to the bathroom. Duke eyed me with curiosity and asked if I was hitting on his friend. The question crashed my operating system.

I was one of those guys who frequented gay nights at Ocidente while in the closet. I'd spent my teenage years suspecting that my near-complete disinterest in girls was the fruit of a combination of timidity and extreme fastidiousness, that the desire I felt for a certain type of man amounted to no more than a pure Apollonian—perfectly intellectual and abstract—appreciation of certain male physical attributes. And women liked me because, with my good manners and decency, I could mask the sensual frustration I felt when sharing moments of physical intimacy with them. I wasn't scared of pussy or any of that moronic nonsense people attributed to gay men. I just didn't see any point in it. The sight of a naked female body didn't excite me. Real women's bodies struck me as even more vulgar and banal than the ones shown in the media—whether in commercials or art—a powerless thing that deserved neither to be revered nor sullied and could therefore hold no real erotic appeal. In any case, I had enough youthful libido in reserve to fulfill the role expected of me as a man. I could go on without questioning myself too much, skirting the dark landscape of my inner instabilities. But when Duke asked if I was hitting on Antero, the look in that son of a bitch's eyes said he could see right through me. It was the first time we were meeting, and it had all lasted mere seconds, yet he already knew me better than I knew myself. And so, instead of denying it, instead of taking his question as just another gay joke between two straight men or a bold-faced jab at my masculinity, as had been the case in the past, I gave him a frank, straightforward response.

"No, he's not my type."

Duke dragged on his cigarette, looked down, flicked the ember onto the floor, and looked at me again.

"What's your type?"

My answer to that question had also been ready for a long time, but only then had I felt free to articulate it to a stranger. My type was more or less me. Large, hairy men with faces cratered from acne or chickenpox. Men with scars, furrows, dandruff. Men who were a little vulgar, gruff, strong, but not too burly. Bricklayers, middleweight fighters, janitors, mechanics. Virile men who desired other men and left no room for effeminacy. Those were the guys I wanted. I didn't often picture myself kissing them or having sex with them, but I had strange fantasies in which I met them in public restrooms and pressed them against the wall, pawing at their husky bodies. I lifted them in my arms, carried, dragged, hoisted them, forcefully leveled and tried to keep them from rising, as in a scuffle between kids or brothers, until they surrendered to me and grabbed at me, too, in rugged jives and complex domination choreographies. That was my type. But just then I didn't have the time to provide Duke with such an elegant answer, so I took a shortcut.

"You're my type."

He wasn't, but what he looked like didn't much matter

in that moment. What mattered was that he'd seen me and had lifted a burden, or a darkness, off my shoulders. When we kissed, I felt the same shudder of disgust as when I had first kissed a girl back when I was fourteen. Then it passed. I became hard. As he drew away from me, Duke asked if I'd like to go home with him. But first he wanted to stay at the party a while longer. He spent hours chatting with other people, avoiding me. I tried to go easy on the beer and instead smoked out the window, drunk on the singularity of my existence.

Around four a.m., we hopped in a cab together. The moment we walked into the living room, he confessed he'd never been with a man before and didn't know how far he could go. A lie, I thought. His statement didn't fit the directness of his approach. In any case, I didn't mention that it was my first time, too. I didn't recognize the apartment as the setting of Antero's film. I'd only find out about that later, from Aurora. We took a few shots of Cachaça Seleta. We blew each other and climaxed while jerking off, then slept together, twisting and turning in his sheets thick with cigarette smoke till the sun began to singe us through his window, bare of curtains or blinds.

After getting up and silently drinking an entire bottle of orange juice between us, half-pretending the other wasn't there, I asked if I could see him again in a couple of days, or the following week, or any other time. He frowned and fiddled with the plastic wrapper on a packet of bread. I noticed the slices had started getting moldy and knew for certain that he'd pick at them later without realizing.

"I'm not gay," he replied.

I felt like punching him in the face. And right then, the penny dropped on just how young he was: a kid sitting on the other end of that Formica table crusty with tomato sauce, wearing yesterday's shirt, crinkled and tucked partway into his jeans. I told him to fuck off and started collecting my things to leave. Duke tried to lighten the mood, claiming that he had enjoyed the experience and, if it were up to him, we'd keep in touch and become friends. In the end, I squeezed his neck affectionately, with a bit more force than necessary, wanting to show him that I was both older and stronger. I said, "I'll see you around, twig," as if in jest. I left, through Old Town and down Rua Demétrio Ribeiro toward the Usina do Gasômetro Cultural Center, half-consoled by the balmy Sunday morning weather in which residents of waterfront town houses were already basking, grills parked on the sidewalk, Lupicínio Rodrigues sounding out from the tape decks of their parked cars. Deep inside I was happy, and yet I knew I'd obsess over Duke for a good while longer, that I would suffer more than necessary, and I did. The sense of loss that encounter sparked in me was unending. Which probably made me just another hopeless romantic. I, who'd so mocked and tortured poor little Manfredo.

Months later, Duke published a story online in which

the reader discovers, in the last few lines, that the first-person narrator who had fallen in love with and fucked a guy was in fact a man and not a woman, contrary to what most readers' biases and prejudices would have led them to expect. It was a bit daft stylistically but also incredibly artful, a narrative feat. And you had to admire the balls on the kid for broaching that kind of topic at a time when sex between men was either invisible or merely hinted at in Brazilian literature and made the hippest of humanities students uncomfortable. He wrote better by the day and did what he had to do. We remained friendly, Duke and I, and you bet I tried sleeping with him again, but he always turned me down gently, with the condescension of liberal, enlightened heterosexuals, so that I was finally able to understand and accept that our one and only intimate encounter had been nothing more than an ironic adventure, just like everything else he and his friends did, the kind of adventure they spent their lives constructing and disseminating with utter conviction, and which with the passing years would become indistinguishable from life itself, and could only end, for him far before the rest of them, with death.

Andrei Dukelski was dead. His path had culminated in the antithesis of adventure, in the least ironic event imaginable. That early dawn, I arrived at the conclusion that it was only after meeting Duke that I became capable of loving someone other than myself, of falling in love. I believed with absolute abandon in the fantasy that this had been his intention from the moment he first approached me, that he had known beforehand all the possible repercussions of our encounter, both for me and himself, and who knows, maybe even for everyone around us. This is what he did. I had loved him, yes, and would forever hold on to the love I'd felt for him. For one fleeting moment of his existence, he had belonged to me and no one else.

I woke up with a hangover and the looming shits, after a night spent in the grips of torturous insomnia and a morning slumber in which I was awoken time and again by the feeling that I was being spied on by the sun. It was just before noon. Before taking a dump, still lying in bed, I lit a Camel, grabbed my cell, and sent Frank a WhatsApp telling him I'd write the book.

As a young Communications student, I used to organize literary soirées where I read my own writing," I said to the audience, which remained invisible while my eyes adapted to the hot, bright bolts from the spotlights. I counted to five before the expected silence. "You were supposed to laugh."

Their laughter echoed through the galleries of São Pedro Theater.

"Thank you, thank you, you're the best. It's true, though, I did organize and participate in my own soirées. This was light-years before blogs or social media. You had to be nifty at programming and possess a sort of trailblazing spirit—key words in today's event—to publish things online. Does anybody here remember ICQ?"

A member of the audience yelped, "Uh-oh!" the notification sound used by that pioneering instant messaging app to announce a new message. Chuckles throughout the theater.

"Awesome, now we're talking," I said, nodding in approval. My eyes finally adjusted to the spotlight, and I could make out the packed seats beneath the theater's prodigious chandelier. Admen, programmers, start-up investors, journalists, trendsetters, creative consultants, cultural entrepreneurs, and humanities students daydreaming of retro beanbags in the game rooms of the creative economy. My talk was the third in that edition of TEDx Porto Alegre, whose gigantic, LED-bulb logo broadcast red light at my back—and I still had more than fourteen minutes, give or take, left onstage. My shirt collar grated on a mole that jutted out from the side of my neck, irritating it. It was long past time for me to schedule a doctor's appointment and put a scalpel to that thing. The stinging snapped me out of focus, and I did the one thing you're never supposed to do in that kind of situation: become a spectator of yourself, glimpse the clown in the arena, see the pithy sadness of it all. A dry cough cruised the perfect acoustics of that neoclassical building. I raised my head and regained my focus. *For some, to try to find and understand value. For others, defining the nature of that value.* The temptation to improvise was taking hold of me.

"One of the pieces I liked reading on those occasions was Marquis de Sade's *The 120 Days of Sodom*. I trust most of you know who de Sade is, and that the cruel, fetishistic eroticism of his texts is what gave rise to the term 'sadism.'"

I pressed the button on the small clicker, activating the next slide, and the tableau of sixteen HD screens was filled with the cover of Aquarius's 1980 edition of de Sade's book, a graphite illustration of a naked, prostrate woman floating in outer space, her arms behind her head and tangled in her wavy hair, her gaping thighs framing a spherical gland that approached her like a sentient planet, contemplating the possibility of penetrating that tuft of pubes. No one laughed; the theater's atmosphere was filled with the far more desirable, yet much more discreet, sound of buttocks shifting in upholstered seats.

"It's quite the little book. De Sade wrote it in 1785 while he was imprisoned in the Bastille. It's the story of four libertine aristocrats who lock themselves up in a secluded mountain castle to—let's say, methodically—put into practice all of their deviances and fantasies. They're accompanied by servants, dozens of tender-aged men and women—all taken by force, of course—and some older, experienced prostitutes whose role is to recount raunchy stories that will stoke the imaginations of those four men."

I paused, glancing back at the book cover on the large screen.

"Right, I could spend hours talking about this book, but I'll try to get to the point. As you might imagine, popping Viagra and toying at porn didn't quite cut if for the four old pals. The *passions* de Sade describes and extols begin with sodomy, coprophilia—i.e., poop—farting on faces, and whipping loins. All just to get warmed up. Then, things get serious. Incest, mutilation, murder. De Sade commemorates the ecstasy of these acts only to, on the same page, sometimes in the same sentence, immediately condemn them as horrific. His contradictions make the text even more uncomfortable. There are various political and philosophical interpretations of this book. It was censured for its immorality, nihilism, and misogyny and simultaneously supported for its libertarianism and decisiveness in our understanding of human nature, even according to feminists like Simone de Beauvoir."

Someone applauded, absurdly.

"But I'm interested in a very specific facet of this book. A question of structure and aesthetics, but also of technology and monetization. Bear with me. *The 120 Days of Sodom* is divided into four parts, dedicated, respectively, to *simple* passions, *complex* passions, *criminal* passions, and *murderous* passions. Each part encompasses no less than *one hundred and fifty* passions or descriptions of sexual acts, spread across thirty days. Go on, use your thinkers to punch those numbers."

I pushed the button again, and the screen displayed a diagram illustrating the book's structure, each part branching into days and each day into passions.

"Here it is." I took the copy of the book from the podium and lifted it above my head. "This is the book. It's a tome, almost four hundred pages long." I opened it and ran my thumb along its pages. "The print is minuscule. It's a large volume, gigantic by today's standards. Now, consider this. The first three hundred pages contain only the first part, the only part de Sade was able to fully develop in prison. Ink was scarce, and he had only a few sheets of paper, glued together to make a scroll. Maybe de Sade knew from the onset that he wouldn't be able to write the entire book. Maybe he was afraid it'd be confiscated. We don't know. The fact is that he filled that scroll with only the first section and then just *sketched out* the three remaining parts, in handwriting as teensy as flea shit, using all the space available to him. This means that the full book, written as he would've wanted, would have amounted to about 1,200 pages of tiny font and cramped spacing. Imagine, then, ye who have not read *The 120 Days of Sodom*, the level of detail with which de Sade narrates his libertines' sexual whims. Consider the obsessiveness of his descriptions, the painstakingness of his structure. Picture, also, the man, in a damp cell in the Bastille of the late eighteenth century, alone with his thoughts and libertine furor, transfixed by hatred and repressed desires, with a plume and a too-short scroll, compulsively writing this book in the space of just thirty-seven days."

In the theater's wings, to my left, the organizer of that TEDx session, a professor of Digital Media at the Pontífica Catholic University of Rio Grande do Sul called Leandra Hmpfelstein, shot me an inquisitive look while pinching the buttons of her blouse. The speech I was delivering was already a far cry from the piece she and the TED specialists had subjected to various interventions—during rehearsals and revisions—in a process that rendered every TED Talk palatable, a slave to their motivational model. The audience silently watched me flip through my copy of the book until I found the relevant pages, marked with neon stick-on flags.

"I'm going to randomly read some of the synopses of scenes de Sade had outlined for the three latter sections of the book, which he didn't have time to develop in full. Passion forty-five: 'He shits in the presence of four women, requires them to watch and indeed help deliver him of his turd; next, he wishes them to divide it into equal parts and eat it; then each woman does a turd of her own. He mixes them and swallows the entire batter, but his shit-furnishers have to be women of at least sixty.'"

Giggles in the audience.

"Another one. Passion eighty-one: 'He has himself flogged while kissing a boy's ass and while fucking a girl in the mouth then he fucks the boy in the mouth while kissing the girl's asshole, the while constantly receiving the lash from another girl, then he has the boy flog him, orally fucks the whore who'd been whipping him, and then has himself flogged by the girl whose ass he had been kissing.' Right, so these are examples of *complex* passions. Now I'll read from the *criminal* and *murderous* passions."

I randomly selected scenes featuring ropes, embers, daggers, and varied forms of debasement. The laughter stopped. The politically correct sensibilities of that audience of innovators couldn't fathom how to respond, and the tension in the air thickened. Leandra shook her head from side to side and gestured for me to stop.

"I think that's enough. My intention here wasn't to shock anyone, partly because it would've been naïve of me to try. On the contrary, the basic argument of this talk is that nothing shocks us anymore. The time when one person could shock another is long gone. What I'd like you to take from de Sade's text is how he discriminates the various elements of his sexual fantasies—each infinitesimal piece of every single thing that excites his imagination—in order to then organize it, mixing and remixing everything ad nauseum. He conceived of no less than six hundred scenes. Though he only had time to flesh out one hundred and fifty of them, he pictured *six hundred* variations of mounting intensity, resorting to a series of recurring elements. This is no ordinary narrative approach. Don't waste your breath trying to find a hero's journey, archetypes, or psychological realism in these pages. What de Sade wrote was an *algorithmic* narrative."

Pressing the button a few more times, I presented a quick succession of images, thumbnails of pornographic videos pulled from the internet.

"De Sade's ideas are maximized through a procedure similar to a combinatorial analysis. More accurately, what the structure of de Sade's novel invokes today is the data processing carried out by computers. Nowadays, we're all so familiar with this logic that we don't even notice it. The pornography that formatted the sexual imagination of my generation, and all those that followed, is produced and disseminated via gigantic databases that hold users' browsing routines and online consumption habits. In consuming internet porn—as everyone here does some way or another—we observe and feed into this logic's production of the erotic. And yet, this same logic extends to all fields of human experience. We also apply it to our own genetic material, to the succession of fad diets and our behavior as spectators and readers, our sleep and work routines, our concepts of happiness. We apply it to scientific research, dating apps, or those apps that count users' steps and heartbeats. We're talking about the *absolute quantification of existence*. We're talking about digitalizing every cultural manifestation imaginable. We treat all our free-world desires in the same way that de Sade, confined between the stone walls of a cell deep inside a castle, treated them."

My time was running out. *For some, the flow of past, present, and future. For others, a single, immutable instant for every possible configuration of the universe.* I rolled up my sleeves.

"Our clients aren't exactly libertines trapped in towers. They're hyper-consumers condemned to be free in an ever-accelerating capitalist world. Digital technology conditions them to convert their desires into information that can be remixed, which leads to the quantification of all things, to the search for the exhaustion of possibility. No human experience, not even art, is free of the jaws of this process. The profanation of all that was once indistinct, inaccessible, and elevated is a *sadistic* process, not in the common sense of the term, meaning cruelty, but in the sense of pining for the methodical exhaustion of desire through data processing."

I kept pressing the button, changing the image on-screen, from a server farm in Silicon Valley to publicity photos inspired by sadomasochism, a genetically modified pig with neon green fuzz, a clip of Lady Gaga, and a bunch of other things chosen at random in a half hour's worth of Google Images browsing. I'd reached the point in my talk where I could show them anything, say anything.

"Out goes intensity, in comes quantity. Out goes the sublime, in come patterns. As de Sade once demonstrated, this doesn't eliminate ecstasy or even beauty, but transfigures them into something else entirely. The beauty that emerges is one of patterns, filing systems, algorithms, montages, and oppositions plucked from an excess of information. In this new world, the possibility of transgressing or transcending doesn't exist. There is no truth slumbering beneath the surface. Flowers that bloom in excess wither from one day to the next."

I allowed the screen to go black for a moment and took another long pause before concluding.

"'Flowers of Excess.' That was the title of this talk. This past year, we worked on a project that proved we could use Marquis de Sade to sell tissue paper. The key words in the ad were 'desire,' 'patterns,' and 'excess.' The commercial only ran late at night on pay-per-view, but our goal from the beginning had been for it to go viral online, without needing to run on TV or any official advertising platforms. Kleenex sales increased by more than forty percent, and now they're miles ahead in the market."

Finally, I pressed play on the minute-long commercial we'd shot for that tissue brand. Several sadomasochistic sex scenes that fused Marquis de Sade–style perversion with the pop softcore of *Fifty Shades of Grey*. Starring in it was Tamara Dalai, an astronomically popular baile funk musician, and a supporting cast meticulously selected from second-rate casting agencies and photography Tumblrs that satisfied standards of beauty that self-defined as nonstandard. The soundtrack was by a post-rock band from the interior of Espírito Santo that had nearly shot to fame after being praised by Radiohead's Jonny Greenwood. The commercial ended with a little product gag, which insinuated that all those people would have to use Kleenex tissues to clean themselves up afterward. The commercial over, I thanked the audience for their attention and received some applause, punctuated by booing. I had never heard of people being booed at a TED event. There was a decent chance my talk would make waves online.

After fleeing my stuffy dressing room in the theater basement—the site of a fierce exchange of business cards, praise, and promises of collaboration that grew in frenzy and senselessness as the AC capitulated and the excess of bodies turned our cramped enclosure into a Dantesque dungeon—I walked down Rua General Câmara to have a beer at Bar Tuim on my own, then caught a cab from Rua Riachuelo to my house, where Giane was waiting for me to babysit Miguel so she could get ready for her night out.

"How'd it go?"

"Well. I went off script a little. Leandra asked about you in the dressing room. They'd like you to give a talk in the next session."

"So long as it's not about girls who play video games, I might just consider doing it," she said in her loud bathroom voice as she waited for the water from the gas-powered shower to heat up. "It'd be good for the company."

Stage fright was Giane's professional Achilles' heel. Though I didn't like to admit it, and would never confess as much to her, it was precisely this weakness that had so impressed me and later compelled me to approach her when I first saw her at a panel on literature and video games at a literary festival in Brasília in the fall of 2008. Her shyness had made it difficult for her to find the right words with which to express her thoughts to the audience, and at her worst her anxiety had seemed to physically crush her. But her ideas were so sound they'd stolen the show anyway. Giane's argument about why video game parameters shouldn't be bound to the narrative sophistication of literature and film—because it drew attention away from the original force of its language, i.e., emerging and procedural narrative—was solid. The other panelists wrinkled their noses when she claimed that plot, quality of dialogue, graphic sophistication, and other such things were secondary and, sometimes, even superfluous in the gaming world; the pleasure and meaning of games lay elsewhere, in interactions, patterns, and rules, in how the processes introduced by them became metaphors for life.

When I approached her after the debate, I blurted out that her ideas on procedural narrative had gotten me thinking. She asked me to elaborate. About what? I didn't have anything good to say. I was just hoping to ask her out for coffee. After I unloaded a bucketful of rubbish all over the poor woman, she was the one left feeling sorry for me. Hearing Giane speak one-on-one—far from the stage, from lenses, and microphones—was like reading an essay that'd gone through three rounds of edits before publication. She spoke how most people dreamed of writing. She was starting her own video game development company that year, and I was considering expanding the use of video games in the marketing activities I cooked up for my clients. We exchanged cards and planned to meet a few days later in Porto Alegre, under the pretext of discussing a possible collaboration. I looked forward to that date more than most things in life. As I headed home, I couldn't stop scanning around the airport, hoping to catch sight of her, and, as I got onto the plane, entertained the dumb fantasy that I'd find her already settled into the seat next to mine. She wasn't there, but she waved at me from two rows back. I squeezed into place, paralyzed, thinking of trying to switch seats, of going to the bathroom at some point during the flight to see if she'd tag along. I didn't do any of that. But we met in Porto Alegre and, just a few months later, were living together.

I entertained Miguel as Giane dried her hair, put on makeup, and got dressed. It had been a long time since she'd managed to plan an evening out with her girlfriends. Miguel embarked on an endless loop whose stages consisted of: bringing me a plastic gorilla, pretending I was a monster who wanted to eat the toy, giggling madly and leaping in fits, fleeing with the toy to the potted pleomele in the corner of the living room, placing the toy on its stalk as if it were climbing, and waiting for me to feign distraction so that he could grab the gorilla again and bring it to me. I tried to encourage this routine as much as possible, hoping Miguel would fall into a self-induced coma before ten o'clock and not wake up until the following morning. I heard the alarm of the taxi app ring in the room and, moments later, saw Giane appear in the living room, a tad ungainly, in flat sandals, a black skirt, and a silk cyan blouse. She leaned over me, took my left nipple between her fingers, and put her lips to my ears.

"I'm going to be feeling wild when I get home."

"I'll leave the straitjacket on the bed."

She left, and for a while I chaperoned Miguel, who started sniveling from sleepiness around ten. The night's unusual goings-on had left him feeling restless. I mashed up a banana for him to eat, checked his diaper, placed him in the crib, and quietly hummed him lullaby covers of

Claudinho & Buchecha's greatest hits until he was deep in the muck of unconsciousness. I looked at him for a while, trying to picture what he was dreaming, if he was dreaming. I remembered having nightmares when I was three or four—feeling I'd been abandoned or that I had been prey to some monster—then waking up terrified and going to sleep beside my parents, who sipped bowls of salmon soup and smoked in bed while I nestled between their legs in a mound of blankets that were thick with their fragrance, a lovely smell that had turned repellent at some point en route to adulthood, like the scent of a stranger. Miguel snored. I pictured him dreaming that a gorilla was trying to bite his face. *For some, madness and dreams. For others, the certainty that madness and dreams are unmistakable phantasmagoria in the face of reality.*

I left the bedside lamp on in the nursery and went to the kitchen for a glass of whisky. I served myself two fingers' worth of single malt and added a splash of cold water. The whisky twisted in oily spirals as the scent of peat and vanilla drifted into my nostrils. The label also mentioned hints of pear and leather, but there was a limit to what I'd let myself pretend to discern. I took the bottle to the living room. I turned on the TV, put it on mute, opened my laptop, and slumped onto the sofa.

I answered a few emails and tried to make a dent in the online articles I'd saved to read over the weekend on an app designed for that purpose, but the television screen showing a GloboNews segment in the background—with images of war, corruption, climate collapse, and urban violence—hijacked my attention. I remembered Aurora's talk of apocalypse on the day of Duke's funeral. If she hadn't been right in front of me, I would have doubted those words had come from her mouth. It was like the difference between a wild animal and a domesticated one. Between a wolf and a bitch that's been shut up in someone's backyard for years. What had happened that night after the funeral had felt like historic reparations, fun and inconsequential, a thing from which we should've emerged feeling lighter. But when we said our goodbyes the following morning, she had seemed even more bitter. Which made it impossible for me to get her off my mind.

I filled my glass with some more whisky and peeked into Miguel's room, even though there was no reason to; he hadn't cried and couldn't have gone anywhere. Leaning against the doorframe, drawing in the scent of childhood emanating from the warm darkness of his room, I thought of how 1999 had been the backdrop of what some might have referred to as pre-millennium tension. Suddenly, the internet and even the pages of the soberest magazines had been rife with articles on Nostradamus's prophecies and the AIs that would one day be a menace to humanity. *For some, faith in the occult. For others, faith in science.* Eschatological superstitions aside, there had been hope back then like never again. The world was still a shitshow, but we floated along in relative calm. I could remember when my dad had gotten the last installment of his retirement savings—which had been confiscated by Fernando Collor de Mello's government and then returned adjusted for inflation—a thing he had doubted would ever happen. The currency had remained stable, and the internet bubble created a sense of future prosperity for the global economy. At the turn of the millennium, the end of the world had been a huge party. Fifteen years later, our greatest enemy, the infamous "millennium bug," seemed like the plot of a subpar sci-fi blockbuster. A mistake in the code—wherein years were recorded in two digits instead of four—that remained present in the minds of most computer programmers, a technicality that could have kicked off system failures across the globe the moment we rang in the year 2000. Of course, fuck all had happened. We had kept drinking and fucking and putting off all manner of professional commitments, as if the future were ours. And our logbook was an e-zine read by thousands of people just like us, half-assed doomsdayers, apocalyptic bungee-jumpers.

Soon after, the Twin Towers fell. A new sense of astonishment welled in me as I stood in my son's room and thought of the weeks and months that had preceded the attack and its consequences. Aurora, Emiliano, Andrei, and I had enacted our own little fake apocalypse. To escape the end of the world, we had spent the turn of the millennium camped out in a secluded ranch that belonged to Emiliano's family, a place somewhere near coal-land, with craggy hills and no electricity or people in sight for kilometers on end. We had raised a glass of cachaça to the apocalypse and roasted lamb in a pit. In the year 2000, New Year's parties around the world had been underwhelmingly ordinary, and the millennium bug was wiped from everyone's memories by New Year's Day hangovers. Fifteen years later, the thing that stretched its tentacles through the limbic systems of grown-up, enlightened people was something else altogether, a different sort of anguish than that of the pre-millennium. This new anguish was the vague prospect of a sluggish and irreversible suffocation, which would be followed by *nothing*. I didn't want to think like Aurora, to be infected by her pessimism. I'd built a good life for myself. I had a successful business and a son to raise. I was a humanist, donating money to community daycare centers and to crowdfunding campaigns for the development of solar panel technology. I believed in the future, in the creative economy, and in capitalism's ability to digest all of its contradictions, even apocalypses. I was convinced the world didn't need saving and that the people who believed as I did would be the ones to save it. It was Tolstoy, I thought, who had said that criminals were the ones who felt certain about what common good was made of; those who thought only of themselves could, inadvertently, change the course of things.

I returned to the living room with vague masturbatory inclinations. My plan was to turn off the TV and try to relax a little with some organic weed I'd gotten from one of my interns who grew his own plants at home, but just then an image on the news stopped me in my tracks. The segment was about a soldier who was standing trial on charges of battery against a kid at the protest against bus fare hikes that had been held in Porto Alegre in June of last year. I focused on the screen and searched for a particular figure that sometimes appeared on the security camera footage being used as evidence in their case. And suddenly there I was, in a red sweat shirt with a T-shirt fastened around my head, concealing my hair and leaving only my eyes exposed, rushing this way and that, leaping over a person who had fallen to the ground, and then finally vanishing offscreen.

When I'd left the office early on the afternoon of the protest, along with some of my employees and interns—their faces painted green and yellow, wielding handmade signs denouncing corruption—I hadn't the least intention of masquerading in black bloc. The protest had started at Paço Municipal, thousands of people gathered under the spray. Umbrellas and colorful rain jackets, coupled with high spirits and a string of placards and chanting, had given our gathering a festival feel, one of celebration more than dissent. At the height of the so-called June Days, demonstrations organized by the Left in protest of the fare hike had morphed into cathartic movements against corruption, the World Cup, the wrongs committed against minorities, and everything else that was fucked up about humanity and our country. Political party banners were shunned, while those wielding them accused the Right of usurping the protest for their bourgeois causes. Even though my heart had been with the voices on the street, my motivation that afternoon was primarily ethnographic. I had wanted to see the march with my own eyes, to watch people and feel their energy on my skin, to capture their desires, dreams, aspirations, and frustrations as accurately as possible. After all, they were our near-future consumers, and it was important for me to understand which products and ideas would best suit their egos and desires. At one point—as protesters sang the anthem of Rio Grande do Sul, a bottle of honey-and-cinnamon-flavored cachaça was passed from hand to hand, and a medley of weed aromas mixed with the scent of wet hair and the filth collected in puddles on the sidewalk—a kaleidoscope of viral videos, hashtags, and media actions that'd tell these people what they wanted to hear about themselves flashed before my eyes. And I already knew which of my portfolio's clients would join ship.

Shortly afterward, still under the rain, the demonstration took on the lethargic tempo of music festival exits. Yet, at the entrance to the Túnel da Conceição, the war cries, handclaps, whistles, and bugles returned full-force, perhaps due to our temporary shelter from the rain or the rather surreal atmosphere in the tunnel, which was magnified by the mustard light from the sodium-vapor lamps and the colorful graffiti covering the walls. A girl with translucent skin, cheeks tinted rose by the cold and hair tied back in a more or less unkempt bun, with a jean jacket over her patterned dress and a purple umbrella in hand, stared fixedly at me as we walked side by side. Everything seemed to point to us knowing each other.

"Are you Antero Latvala?" she asked. "From *Orangutan*?"

I assented and drew near her. Her wet cheeks and forearms were spattered with green and yellow glitter. She was marching with two friends, whom I was introduced to in a brief exchange of nods.

"You look too young to have been an *Orangutan* reader."

"I was fourteen. I subscribed to it on the seventh issue or so."

The demonstration left the tunnel and continued along Sarmento Leite. Residents threw ticker tape at the protesters and played vuvuzelas from their apartment windows. The girl opened her umbrella, one of its ribs broken, and offered me shelter. Already soaked through, I accepted. There was a tattoo of a constellation on the nape of her neck. One of her friends presented me with a plastic container filled with cake.

"It's vegan," her friend said.

"Good to know," I said, reaching for a piece. My wedding ring flashed, and silence lingered in the air. The girl's other friend was photographing the march and, every so often, drew away from the group to capture scenes such as that of a bearded, made-up man in a ballerina outfit offering a policeman a flower or a girl on a unicycle posing with a sign denouncing abuses by FIFA and the Belo Monte Dam.

"Wow, I used to freaking love your pieces. And your hair's still long! Just like in the photos you all had on the website."

"Those photos would get us locked up nowadays."

"You were always naked in them. It was hilarious. Your family's from Iceland, right?"

"Finland. My great-grandparents emigrated to Brazil in the 1930s."

"Ah, right. You wrote some amazing pieces about their history."

It was incredible that she remembered those things. The pieces she was referring to, like the many others I'd published online in the nineties, had for years been stuffed into the very back of my memory and felt like they'd been written by someone that I had no doubt once been and yet had long stopped being. At eighteen, I'd hitchhiked to Penedo, in Rio de Janeiro, to retrace my great-grandparents' footsteps on their arrival to Brazil. The history of Finns in that city was well-documented, both in museums and through stories that lived on in the community. My great-grandparents had landed in Brazil with a wave of immigrants who were seeking a utopian life, closer to nature. It wasn't long before the Finnish colony went into crisis, unable to sustain itself on family agriculture alone. But the year he'd arrived, my great-grandfather, a skilled joiner who'd never adapted to the community's hippie ethos, had gone looking for other locales in which to set up home. He and my great-grandma turned up in Rio Grande do Sul with their only son, rudimentary Portuguese, and not a penny to their name. From what I gathered, they had lived in the mountains for a while before settling in Porto Alegre. This part of their story was a bit nebulous, but in the late 1940s, my grandfather, who'd married a young woman from the region, opened a small hardware store in the Azenha neighborhood of Porto Alegre. When he died of pneumonia, devastated by the city's humid climate, my father took over the business. At first, he had only two small storefronts and two employees. A natural-born businessman, in just two decades he turned the small Latvala Hardware store of Azenha into a chain of superstores that sold tools and construction material. I had published three pieces on their history in *Orangutan*, strategically sentimental anecdotes spliced with the account of my ego-tripping journey to Penedo, in which I tried to titivate my family's history with the duplicitous intention of, at the end of the third piece, ragging on the political conservatism of my parents and grandparents, not to mention my great-grandfather, who had cowardly fled a socio-utopian experiment in the Serra Fluminense. Now that I had a business and a family of my own, it hurt to think of the time I had scoffed at their lives for the sake of scoring points with my readers.

By then, the march was running down Avenida João Pessoa toward Avenida Ipiranga. Our final destination, the girls said, was the corner of Avenida Erico Veríssimo, right in front of the *Zero Hora* newspaper headquarters. Policemen on horses galloped alongside the protest as if guiding a herd through the valley between buildings. A municipal garbage container spat out smoke and tall red flames. Just then, I was overcome by a feeling of anguish of uncertain origin and considered heading home. I asked the girl for her name, which she gave me. I forgot it that same night, never to remember it again. I also asked for her number. And she asked why my wife hadn't joined me at the protest.

"You're right, I'm sorry," I said, and walked quickly through the crowd until I was sure I had left them all behind. I felt like setting something on fire or swiping a gun from a cop's holster, just so I could face the consequences. At a clip, I reached the corner far earlier than expected. And from that moment on, everything was a blur. The cops guarding the headquarters charged the front line of protesters. The concussion from the tear gas and flash bombs was followed by a swathe of smoke and screams. Some of the protesters retreated to Avenida da Azenha, where the sound of smashing glass marked the transition from peaceful protest to something else altogether, a few degrees' escalation in the violence and unrest. This was when a strange idea occurred to me. In a matter of minutes, the riot would reach my dad's shop. The original Latvala storefront. The shop my grandfather had opened in that same spot in 1940s Azenha after abandoning the impoverished Finnish colony in Penedo with his family and traveling south to Porto Alegre in search of better opportunities and colder climes. My father had taken that first shop, a modest consignment store, and over the course of decades built the Latvala family emporium, which now boasted seven locations in greater Porto Alegre and two in Santa Catarina. "Construction Proud," that was our motto. I looked around. A handful of masked protesters were ransacking the motorcycle dealer on the corner.

I pulled off my red sweatshirt, wet with rain, and my gray shirt, strapped the latter around my head and pulled on my sweatshirt again. I ran toward the store, two blocks ahead. A group of half a dozen masked protesters used a wooden trestle as a battering ram to shatter the shop window of a branch of Banco do Brasil. Someone approached me and doused the shirt around my face with vinegar. I felt twenty years old again, drunk on my covert performance. It was as if the site of that conflict were a sophisticated virtual reality simulator plugged in for my convenience. The simulation was improbably realistic, yet what stuck with me most of all was the noise. Flash bombs exploding; the sonic drilling of military brigade sirens, whose volume and frequency were designed to cause the utmost mental distress to everyone in range; the low gargling of propellers from the press helicopter overflying the protest; terse yells from protesters communicating in groups, either alerting or orienting those who were or should have been on their side of the scuffle; cops' and protesters' stampeding boots and sneakers brushing the asphalt and treading hither and thither, making a gravelly noise; shards of glass from the windows of shops and parked cars; chants from the packs of protesters at the intersection with Avenida Ipiranga, only a few dozen meters from the fracas with the cops and the looters; protesters trying to distance themselves from a violence that frightened and baffled them; barks of warning and fear from dogs kept in plots that were still mid-construction and in residential patios tucked in the heart of the neighborhood; the sound of the light rain that hadn't stopped falling since late afternoon; the strangely muted and dull thump of kicks, punches, rocks, sticks, and the like striking human bodies, as if they were made not of flesh but cardboard; the soft crack of a forearm radius or ulna snapped like a toothpick by a baton just meters away, click, leaving the victim's hand suspended at the point of fracture. I hurled chunks of sidewalk against car windows. Why? There was no adequate response. I was an extra, an NPC. I required no motivations and shrugged off the limelight. I was in my own simulator; there would be no consequences. I didn't intervene when they smashed my father's shop window, the store with my name on the sign. They swiped tools, handsaws. Let them take it. In the heat of the moment, the righteousness of it seemed clear as day. Standing there, I thought of how the security cameras were filming everything. I knew the location of every camera in the shop. I knew I'd feature in those images, though in that moment I couldn't have foreseen that I'd become an extra on news clips, rushing through the background of the scene of a crime, forever incognito. Because no one on the face of the planet would have ever imagined that I would be there.

The news program ended. The opening segment of a broadcast on the economy sopped up the echoes of my black bloc cosplay. I carelessly finished rolling a spliff and smoked it while compulsively clicking through the photo albums of women I didn't know and yet was friends with on Facebook. I felt the call of the wank. I would never apologize, not to anyone. I was who I was, did what I did. *For some, all that exists. For others, mutually exclusive alternatives.* I filled my glass halfway with single malt and opened the landing page of my favorite porn website. I tucked an earbud into my left ear and left the right unobstructed so that I could hear Miguel crying or Giane's unlikely early return. I scanned thumbnails of recent additions, scouring for details that even I wouldn't have been able to put into words, a face, a gaze, a dick penetrating an ass in a way that jibed perfectly with tactile and visual predilections that were rooted in my very being. I combed through the site's first half dozen pages, selecting videos and opening them in separate tabs with a ctrl+click so they would load in the background while I continued my research. I then selected pages at random from the video timeline, trying my luck on slightly older posts, which always seemed to contain gems poised to slip past me. The videos I was after had to fulfill a rather complex set of criteria. There should be white male performers like me, and no more than two or three of them. The man on film, when not shot in the first-person, had to be someone I could project myself onto completely, to the point of fully replacing him in the film's action, which is why any glaring differences had to be eliminated. No girls who looked remotely adolescent or prepubescent. Definitely no prostheses, not on any body part. No ludicrous costumes or intricate contextual scenarios, such as wives sold for cash, cuckolding, or mother-daughter storylines. No extreme hardcore, humiliation, rectal prolapses, fucking machines, or spit-puking. Points were awarded for casual S&M, ropes and collars, gags, asphyxiation. The scenario I was after was of women submitting voluntarily as objects and men with maximum visibility, a sort of diagrammatic sexual intercourse devoid of all sophistication. I wanted excitable triggers of Pavlovian efficiency. Models with healthy, attractive bodies exploring the limits of their species' lubrication and motor skills with performative diligence and credible abandon; with spasms and liquids and eyes turned skyward, and that silent cry—frozen in ecstasy and agony—of certain actresses in climax that could make the entire cosmos stop for the few seconds it took for the cum to tickle the root of the testes and splurge into the Marquis de Sade Kleenex.

After an initial jaunt through recent video pages, the time came to select a few categories and probe them one by one—the cursor lingering over the thumbnail, making the mini-preview of the scenes pop up—until I came across something promising. I narrowed it down to the following categories: squirting, ebony+teens, russian, and amateur. I opened three to four videos in each category in separate tabs. By the time I had wrapped up this stage, the videos in the first few opened tabs would have finished loading. I proceeded to stream each one of the videos in opening order, clicking on the progress bar to scan through scenes, searching for the best moments. Perfect moments that were difficult to find and had a certain ineffable quality about them, but which gradually composed a narrative that made sense to me as an imaginary fuck. The scenes selected weren't necessarily the most exciting, aesthetically pleasing, or well-executed; on the contrary, they were nearly always unflattering to the actors' bodies or technically clumsy. They corrupted the pristine content of my imagination. I wasn't after decals of my own fantasies but rather images that trod over my imagination with the filthy soles of their shoes. Most of the preselected clips didn't pass muster and were closed. Half an hour later, I'd hit on a series of a dozen videos that were paused at the exact scene or instant approved by my onanistic aesthetic vision.

I cracked my knuckles and neck. I got up to check on Miguel and went to the kitchen for a glass of water to relieve my dry tongue. I returned, poured myself another whisky, and started arranging the videos in small, uniform windows that filled the desktop with a mosaic of scenes that could be triggered in the exact order I had anticipated. From the chaos of digital fuckery, I'd birthed a work of art that would exist for the space of my glorious toss-off, only to then be wiped away forever, like a Tibetan sand mandala. I lit my blunt, took a couple of deep drags, and then began pressing play on each video in the premeditated sequence, working my cock to the rhythm of the action. I was soon sweating and pulled off my shirt. At certain moments, I would use the trackpad to rewind to the beginning of a particular scene, until I was satisfied with that stage and ready to move to the next video. Sometimes, sticking my fingers up my ass seemed inevitable, and so I would half-stand, half-sit, close to coming yet still able to refrain and keep on, stringing together the streaming fragments, touching and groping the trackpad as if it were a sensitive fabric, moving my haunches in synch with the performer eating out the ass of a brunette clad only in ripped pantyhose, squatting on the floor, mascara running down her cheeks, lapping up milk from a saucer. Sweat ran down my chest and belly, and my knees started aching. I stuck my spit-slicked finger up my tail again, like my dear Giane sometimes did, her tapered little fingers homing in on my prostate, a target I couldn't risk reaching on my own. I still had the three or four final scenes of the sequence to trigger, but a moment came when I couldn't take it any longer and reached for the wad of tissues I had left on the coffee table so I could climax without soiling the entire living room, while simultaneously expelling a grunted litany of curses and moans. My pleasure arrived with the instant frustration of a solitary climax, which is a bit like waking up from an erotic dream to the pathetic scene under way. I was overcome by a deep lassitude and a slight nausea from the booze. *For some, sensual pinnacles. For others, the abyssal depth of quashed desires.* I hadn't made it to the last clips of my cinematic masterpiece, which included two stunning facials, and the slight emptiness left by this unfinished narrative grew all the more sorrowful in the face of the modest seminal emission I'd attained after so much effort and abandon.

I spent a while sitting in the armchair, waiting for my cock to soften, my urethra smarting a little. I closed all the windows and tabs. I checked the time in the corner of the screen and saw that over an hour had passed. All my life's contradictions boiled down to an insipid, inoffensive slime. I pricked up my ears to check if Miguel was making any noise. For a moment, I heard only the stereophonic sounds of cars driving past on the street below. After a moment of utter silence, a spectacular rainfall began. The crackling of fat drops hitting the tin of the AC unit hanging outside the living room window soon gave way to the frothy sound of thick rain flogging the asphalt, the trees, the cars. Thunder roared in the distance.

I hitched up my pants and hauled my quaking legs down the hallway to the bathroom. I removed the child seat we had been using to teach Miguel to poop on the toilet and pissed with satisfied moans. I washed off my dick in the shower so I wouldn't stink of cum. I walked into the nursery. My son slept as if nothing at all had happened. When Miguel had been born, a translucent babe with a little Finnish head atop his body, he had looked a lot like my dad. At two and a half, he was more like his mom, or, rather, like her brother, a successful hyperrealist painter who had pronounced eyebrows and looked a bit like Mastroianni. If his mother had any say in it, though, the kid wouldn't grow up to be an artist. Giane had plans for the boy. She would foster an interest in mathematics, immerse him from an early age in technology, and guide him surreptitiously toward computer sciences and engineering. Miguel was already playing with apps on his iPad that stimulated his pup-brain. Giane talked about teaching him Krav Maga, family farming, sustainable construction. These were all just projections, though, and I knew she wouldn't force all of that on the boy. And yet, it was impossible not to see how, unconsciously, she seemed to want to prepare him for a world far different from the one we had been raised in. A world where resources were scarce and the few jobs still available involved designing and supervising the machines that would look after the rest of the world.

The green LED on my cell blinked in slow motion. I unlocked it and saw a notification for a missed call. Aurora had rung while I'd been jerking off. I shivered at the thought that she might still be in Porto Alegre so long after the funeral, or that she'd gone back to São Paulo but for some reason wanted to talk to me, and so late at night. It was after midnight, Giane might show up at any moment, but I called her back anyway. Aurora didn't answer. I waited five minutes and tried again, no luck. Then again. The screen of the still-muted TV showed endless commercials for the network's own programs, making the entire living room flicker with epileptic light. When I turned it off, the noise from the rain seemed to have grown louder. For a few minutes, I remained suspended in that empty moment, tuned in to the many soft, invisible forces around me. The objects keeping me company in the living room exerted a microscopic gravitational force on me, as if watching me, until suddenly I began to imagine that they, like I, also possessed some sort of inner life. Together we—me, Andrei Dukelsky's novels on the shelves, the coffee table, my son's myriad toys scattered across the rug and armchair, the Tiffany table lamp, the fern Giane had brought with her from her old apartment, and Araki's Polaroid—were waiting for that moment to be interrupted by another phone call from Aurora, one in which she'd tell me what she wanted or inform me of something I couldn't have foreseen, destroying what had already been cemented between us. She shouldn't mean anything to me; I'd assured myself she'd be easy to forget and tried to think of her as just a friend of fifteen years, and yet there I was again, reminiscing on that late night in the A2 motel where we'd gone after drinks at Sabor Um, after Andrei's funeral, the same motel I'd taken girls to back in our *Orangutan* days. Thinking of how we'd fucked drunk as all hell, trying to enact how it might have been when we were twenty years old.

She'd looked down on me in our e-zine days and still looked down on me now after all those years. I knew that the reason she'd wanted to open her legs to that derision was that Andrei had been killed, because life was shit and the future had at some point ceased to exist, and it was all too late now. In the entire time we had spent together in that room, she'd barely looked me in the eyes, moaning somewhat theatrically, time and again seeking out our reflection in the rusted, steamy mirrors decorating the ceiling and walls. She was bitter and scared. I was swollen with a sense of retribution. I was married, and she knew it. In a nutshell, everything was wrong and, for that same reason, everything was right. It was one of those situations for which sex seemed custom-made, to create a fleeting shelter for something wrong that we nonetheless needed, and so we had fucked with rage and gratitude until we were squalid and dog-tired. I remembered my hands grabbing her ass, Aurora belly-down on the mattress, round and hard, arching her spine and shoulders. As I admired the supple contortions of her back, thick droplets of blood started crashing onto her golden skin, like a hallucination in a psychological thriller. Catatonic, I watched the droplets morph into red filaments that began to form puddles in the furrows of her back, and only then did I bring my hand to my face to check for a nosebleed.

"My nose is bleeding."

Aurora hadn't understood. She'd thought I'd been hissing something lewd through my teeth and so grunted an incentive in response. I stopped penetrating her and repeated that there was blood coming out of my nose. She hadn't noticed anything and was taken aback when she turned her head to look at me. My eyes searched for the mirror on the headrest and glimpsed my bloodied mouth and chin.

"Fuck, what's wrong, are you all right?"

"Fine, my nose just started bleeding, I don't know. This has never happened before."

"I'm filthy."

We looked at each other for a moment, our eyes wide open, our breath suspended. In my facial muscles I felt a childish smile caught at my lips.

"It's like that scene in *Angel Heart*," she said, more sarcastic than enthused.

"Yes," I agreed, elated, holding my nose and lifting my head a little. It was a good scene. Mickey Rourke with Lenny Kravitz's wife, blood raining from the ceiling. My cock throbbed to the rhythm of my heartbeat and seemed about ready to drop off. "The cleaning staff's going to have plenty to think about."

I went to wash up in the bathroom and came back with a wad of toilet paper under my nose and another to wipe her off.

"It's like in Japanese anime, you know, when the dude gets aroused and blood starts gushing from his nose."

"OK," she said, and I realized it'd be a mistake to try to turn that one episode into a sort of spiritual connection between us, at least right then. Aurora couldn't be bothered with that kind of thing. I hadn't cum yet, which had become critical, so I shut my mouth and started slowly eating her out, until things were back on track. Minutes later, she assured me that I could cum inside her and that's what I did, my entire cock buried in her, unmoving, both hands at her neck, not squeezing so much as holding, feeling on my palms and fingers all the ducts and tendons beneath her fine skin. The motel's complimentary condoms lay intact on the cold floor, and again I asked myself what had become of the panic over AIDS and venereal diseases, which in college had people eating pussy through plastic film.

Only after showering, as we zipped up our pants to leave, did Aurora do something that could be construed as affectionate, running her fingers through my hair.

"So, you haven't cut your hair short since back then?"

I said no. She couldn't contain a small, senseless smile, the smile of a person simply contemplating the passage of time, and then immediately sniffed at her wrists.

"Motel soap. It'd been a while."

"Only water for me," I said. "Safer that way."

"Right."

"I think I'll walk a bit, then hop in a cab."

"Good idea. I'm still drunk. Fair chance I might crash or be pulled over in a sting."

We left the motel in her car, I paid the bill, like any decent guy would have back in the day, got out on Rua José de Alencar, and walked along Avenida Érico Veríssimo, nearly all the way to Avenida Ipiranga, where I climbed into a cab and went home. We didn't speak again, not even on Facebook, where now and then I saw her online. It was awful, and yet I couldn't get out of my head the moment when she'd run her fingers through my hair, nor the slight smile that had followed. That stilled moment pointed to a wistful past, and it was awful because we weren't the kind of people who thought of the past in that way. I wanted her there with me on that sofa, naked like that night at the motel but free of remorse, little by little conceding me some affection.

The key turned in the lock outside the living room door.

I was so lost in thought that I hadn't heard the sounds of the elevator or the footsteps coming down the hallway. Giane came into the house as she usually did, leaving the door wide open behind her and then turning around to shut it, as if she'd forgotten. She closed the door, took off her shoes, and walked toward me on the sofa.

"I'm wet."

She bowed her head, letting her amber hair, wet with rain, brush my face. I reached out my arms and set my hands on her waist.

"How was it?"

"It was great," she said quietly, her voice languid. "There were these pomegranate cocktails. Mônica is moving to Belgium in May, I had no idea. An artists' scholarship. We talked about leaving Brazil. All of them have an exit plan for after the World Cup. Lari's going to be a call girl in Portugal, she's already got hold of Cristiano Ronaldo's number. Suzana and Beto are going to Israel, his mother is Jewish."

"And where are we going?"

"How about Canada? They need people, and there's a strong gaming industry there. Also, I like the cold and the snow."

"Canada it is. Or Finland."

"Canada. They'll like my game there."

She meant a project she had been developing on her own for three years now, alongside the dozens of commissioned games that kept her business afloat. A super bizarre, experimental game in which a player controlled various objects, from simple things such as balls and chairs to complex equipment like fans and tractors. On my most recent visit to the studio, I'd seen an alpha version playing on a computer and been left speechless. It was lovely and mysterious, seemingly aimless and senseless. In it, you could travel with objects between faraway worlds that looked like small planets endowed with *Super Mario Galaxy* gravity, yet its graphic style was eclectic, evoking older games from the 8- and 16-bit era. It was intimidating to see Giane working on this while managing a team of thirty people in the production of simpler, more conventional games. She showed me her meticulous game design schedule, colorful charts in which the games' mechanics came to life so they could then be coded by programmers, illustrated by artists, and animated by animators. Her team—men and women with backgrounds in industrial design, visual arts, computer sciences, and architecture, as well as autodidacts in 3-D modeling and programming language—was drawn to her like a moth to the flame, inside a vast, open-plan studio space decorated with posters featuring characters from the company's creations, cartoonish critters and brutes in futuristic armor. The work she did was as creative as mine, but the creativity involved in hers was of a different nature, digital and refined, a kingdom of precision and elegance. My work thrived on impurity and dishonesty. Any twit who'd ever written a novel or directed a film liked to claim that art couldn't exist without honesty, that lies and simulation simply harkened to an underlying truth. To them, I would say that dishonesty at its purest was the aesthetics of the future. Almost nobody got this. Giane certainly didn't. When I spoke to her about my job, she listened attentively and respectfully, nodding her head a little as if generously ignoring a boil on my cheek.

"Canada, then. Wherever you like."

She sat on my lap. I hugged her, but I was stiff. I could feel it.

"Did Migs go to bed early?"

"He only passed out around ten, but he hasn't woken up since."

"Is everything all right, Antero?"

"I think so. Just kind of tired."

"You stink of whisky. Whoever wakes up with the milder headache gets to take him to school tomorrow morning. I'm going to brush my teeth and lie down."

I heard her walk into the kitchen, fill a glass with tap water, and drink it, then go into Miguel's room, from which she didn't emerge for approximately three minutes. She peed, brushed her teeth, took off her clothes, and fell into bed. I stayed in the living room a tad longer, then went straight to the room and lay down. She woke up, threw her leg over my waist, and kissed me on the neck and chest. She dug her hand between her legs, beneath the duvet, and started dipping her fingers in her cunt.

"Can you hear me?" she asked.

"Yes."

She removed her hand from between her legs and placed her slicked-up fingers in my mouth. Then she turned her back to me, slipped the duvet down to her knees and ground her ass against my cock. Together, her thighs, hips, and abdomen formed a flexible, aerodynamic whole, like a thing sculpted from wind that was coming to life. But after several glasses of whisky and an epic wank, followed by a sharp moral shock, I was more like a boneless chicken and could think only of why Aurora had called and then not answered her phone, and was riddled by the rare and awful but not unfamiliar feeling that Giane was superior to me, that she was fairer, more talented, cleaner, and that her mere existence was an affront I wasn't prepared to suffer, and the resentment that sprang from this made me think that her body, flabbier and puffier by the day, wasn't as attractive as it had been when we'd first met, before she'd had Miguel, which made me think of the interns at my agency and the dozens of women I stalked on social media and exchanged nude pics with on my cellphone, and floating above all that muck was the image of my dad's shop being torn apart by rioters and the somewhat unreliable memory that I myself, for god knows what reason, had hurled something at the shop window. *To some to others blah blah blah.* I wished my son would wake up crying in the night to rescue me from that quagmire, and I tuned in to the quiet in the apartment, as if I could rouse the boy by will alone, or as if my affliction could reach him through the ether that existed between fathers and sons. But none of it was necessary in the end, because Giane began to lose steam and wilt until, finally, she turned to face me, whispered "OK," sighed, and fell asleep with dreadful ease.

Nobody wanted to see the horror of abundance, of things brimming over and proliferating until bursting. The horror that emptiness could inspire in the human soul was comforting next to the horror of things and beings swarming. What I felt as I walked the paved length of Largo da Batata on that Friday morning—from the bus stop to an address on a little street in Pinheiros, where I'd get an abortion—was a kind of horror. It had rained not long ago, and the gutters still guzzled down the grayish stew that streamed off the curb. I would have to zigzag at random to move through the crowd, like a cockroach in flight, never stopping. It was imperative not to stop. Or so Mr. Gregório, the University of São Paulo driver who used to take me to the cane fields in Araras, had taught me. He practiced Hinduism and traveled to India once a year to study and meditate with his teacher. The best way to cross an avenue in Mumbai, he said, was to always move diagonally and not stop under any circumstance. This method worked both for people and vehicles. For cockroaches and rats.

A rat was a fine creature, when seen in isolation, independent of other rats or their relation to diseases and historic plagues. Soft and curious, clever in its own right and ferocious when under duress, the rat invited admiration. But at a certain degree of concentration, horror bloomed. The sight of thousands of rats devouring one another in the hold of an abandoned ship adrift at sea was repulsive, worthy of horror films. The infestation of any living organism could provoke horror in the hearts of men and women. Any organism. If you herded enough butterflies into a crowded space, soon the simmering density of their bellies and the bristling of their wings would stand your hairs on end and turn your stomach. There was no reason it should be different with humans. We had infested the planet, or at least the streets of São Paulo. One of the traits of a living organism, philosophically speaking, was self-interest, and it was the intense concentration of these self-interests that turned crowds nauseating. Mob violence, rallies, and rock concerts could upend that logic, but on the streets of São Paulo that Friday morning, there existed only terror and the feeling that it just couldn't be, that something must have gone wrong for there to be so many people trying to go about their lives in the same place. Human proliferation was in itself a constraint on humanity, I thought. Our entire species seemed destined to win itself a cosmic-scale Darwin Award for the feat of attaining self-extinction through improved life expectancy. Soon, there wouldn't be space or food enough in the ship's hold, and the rats would start devouring one another. That is, of course, unless scientists like me conjured a new Green Revolution. Space agencies were researching the viability of colonizing planets similar to ours. To colonize, we would have to eat. To eat, we would have to sow. To sow, we would have to figure out how to make plants grow in a new photoperiod, under another sun and with another understanding of night and day, of seasons, of etc. Hi, pleased to meet you, my name is circadian rhythm, what's yours? But it was becoming increasingly clear to me that miracles, the kinds on afternoon TV movies, as well as so-called "scientific miracles," were simply a condition for the emergence of a new and more serious set of problems. "Scientific miracle." The kind of notion that lifted Antero's spirits.

I had taken two drugstore tests after a week-late period, both of which had come out positive, and gotten up twice at dawn to pee. On the night I took the second test, I rang Antero, and he didn't answer. I'd been ready to inform him of the situation, as dryly and directly as possible. I hadn't taken the pill properly the week of Andrei's death, while visiting my parents. I only realized this much later. Antero would be angry, but what could you do, sometimes I just forgot, and the string of incidents that week had messed with my head and with my routine. Once Antero absorbed that first piece of news, I would unceremoniously notify him of my decision to have an abortion, which I expected him—because of his family situation and the kind of man he was—to immediately agree to, or almost, because first he'd probably ask me if I was absolutely sure, or something along those lines. As I used my fingertip to press the small, androgynous photo icon of Antero in my cell's contact list, my plan was to travel to Porto Alegre to get an abortion. I pictured Antero going with me to the clinic and participating in the entire process. He was the father, after all.

He didn't answer, and I didn't dial him again. Instead, I stared at the icons on my iPhone until they dissolved in my eyes. Behind them was a background photograph of my sugarcane plants on the Araras campus of the University of São Carlos, their brown internodes and green leaves gleaming in the sunset, bathed in orange light vivid as embers. I'd been preparing myself for a new defense since early March, and it would take place in three weeks, in the first half of April. Nothing too complicated. The truth was my project was solid, as were its findings, and this time César wouldn't be on my evaluating committee, so he couldn't sabotage me. I thought of all the years I had devoted to my research, and of my move to São Paulo, a city that crushed me with its excesses, with its anthill-density, its sickening stench of hot asphalt, and its inhuman atmosphere of cordial competitiveness. I thought of my lonely evenings and of the daily bus rides from Santa Cecília to the University of São Paulo. What could Antero have to do with all of that? He didn't know a thing about me and wasn't the least bit capable of understanding what I did, he in his little life as an adulterous adman from a well-to-do family, flushed and full of himself, a sardonic smile always burgeoning between babyish cheeks that had swelled with the passing years, cruising on the winds of the alt social capital he'd amassed since youth. Neither his undeniable creative vigor nor his sexual magnetism had any business in my world or with my temperament. Why, then, should he come with me to the abortion clinic? How did an episode of accidental fertilization turn him into a partner, an accomplice? He was a friend, sure, so he could go ahead and shower me with all the support and affection warranted in that kind of situation—he could even be an active father, or at least help me financially if I were to end up having the kid—but how could he fathom the twelve-hour days that I spent extracting RNA from hundreds of sugarcane tissue samples, the bimonthly urinary infections I got from being chained to my workbench, not even getting up to go to the bathroom, stumbling home with just enough energy to slap together a sandwich with whatever I had in the fridge and watch half an episode of *Mad Men* on my laptop before passing out, drooling, on the sofa, socializing with only my adviser and lab colleagues for months at a time, people who were generally pleasant to interact with and with whom I shared a handful of interests but who were nonetheless as consumed by their research as I was? It would be embarrassing, still, to try to explain to him that even if the world weren't on a path to destruction, a person like me was in no condition to raise a kid on her own, maybe not even with somebody else; that all I could hope for was to find a partner and start a family of professional colleagues capable of understanding and handling that routine, with all its particular demands; that the ethidium bromide I used to dye DNA during electrophoresis lab procedures held significant risks and could cause gametogenesis and malformations in the gametes; and that this was only one of the many mutagenic, flammable, and toxic compounds I was surrounded by every day, which made gestation itself a rather hazardous undertaking.

And why travel to Porto Alegre just to get rid of a fetus? It was an instinctual response and nothing else. Porto Alegre was the place I was born, where my parents lived, my roots. Subconsciously, Porto Alegre was still where I returned to in moments of weakness, the one place on the planet that would welcome me back under any circumstance. But none of this could stand up to a more rational analysis. The city was more unsafe now than ever before, and my ties to it had, in the last few years, lost all meaning. It'd been a long while since I'd had anything to discuss with my friends there; even the urge to share silly clips with them via chat was long gone. The green dots beside their names on Facebook and Gmail were just enough to keep up the appearance that we'd once been close and still mattered to each other. Obviously, I couldn't breathe a word of it to my parents, whom I knew to be "pro-life," in the obscurantist, atavistic, hazily religious, and scientifically ignorant sense of the term. I had in me—or at least within a few kilometers of where I stood—everything I needed to handle the situation, except, perhaps, money, if in the end the clinic charged more than my measly doctoral grant could cover. If I couldn't afford a decent clinic on my own, I'd ask Antero to contribute. But if I could subsidize it solo, there was no reason I shouldn't get an abortion by myself, right in São Paulo, without discussing it with Antero or with anyone else. It was in the middle of that train of thought that my cellphone started ringing. Antero, returning my call. It was after midnight, and I could picture him seeking out a discreet spot from which to speak to me, far from his wife's ears. He hadn't taken off his wedding ring when he had fucked me after Andrei's funeral, either because he'd been too drunk or because he hadn't cared. The gold ring had shone on his finger as he pinched his nose to stop the bleeding, his face marred by that manic expression children get when they've eaten too much sugar. The AC had chilled my back, drenched with blood and sweat, and all I could think of was telling him not to stop, to fuck me more and just keep bleeding, that I liked blood—but what sort of a deranged bitch would he think I was—so I had gone and washed myself off instead. And then I wanted more. I wanted it so much. It'd been some time since I'd been properly screwed. He asked me again and again if I was on the pill, and I gave him the answer that wouldn't interfere with things. It was an honest answer, too—I did think everything was all right. I wasn't trying to fool anyone, I just needed to cum with a cock for once.

I let the phone ring until he gave up, after three tries. After the device finally went quiet, I was able to make out the elated yelling of people drinking in bars on the street behind my building. I took a deep breath to stop from crying, but everything was all right, it was all right, I told myself insistently. It was less a matter of sadness than relief.

The next morning, before heading to USP, I called my gynecologist and scheduled an appointment for Tuesday. When I reached my laboratory office, I called her secretary again and cancelled the appointment. I'd been seeing Dr. Nívea for three years and had no complaints; she'd given me the right medications for cramps and cystitis and had doled out antibiotic prescriptions with comforting ease. What frightened me most just then was Dr. Nívea's quasi-maternal complicity: that robust, fifty-year-old woman with her firm, warm handshake, black hair always pulled back scalp-tight, and lips painted red. Especially when the issue at hand was a pregnancy termination. The tone she used during our consultations was more that of a sexologist for teenagers than of an adult, enlightened woman whom one might take as an accomplice in life's thornier issues. She always asked if I was having safe sex and resorted to childish euphemisms such as "down there" and "a roll in the hay." She gave me the impression that, however competent a doctor she might be, she held a misogynistic view of women as reproductive creatures and slaves to their hormones, and that she believed in an idyllic world in which sex could be a fully consensual human interaction, planned for and safe, in which nothing could go wrong—so long as there was information, good faith, respect, and the right moral inclination. My gut said it was a mistake to discuss abortion with her. The danger in it was, precisely, that she might treat me too empathically when all I wanted was an address jotted down on a piece of paper.

Another option was to buy a fistful of Cytotec pills at fifty reals a pop from a street vendor on Rua 25 de Março, leave them under my tongue for thirty minutes, swallow them, and wait for the ensuing cramping and bleeding that would either put an end to matters or, at the very least, ensure I was taken care of in a hospital. Though it was the cheapest and most discreet option, I just couldn't handle it.

I switched on my prehistoric workbench computer, a yellow PC I referred to as Tamagotchi, opened an anonymous browser, and Googled abortion procedures. At some point Sabrina—the postdoctoral researcher I shared an office with—arrived, and I had to close the browser window. I opened another, logged on to Facebook, and started scrolling through my list of friends displayed onscreen. There was Rita, a high school friend who'd had an abortion in her junior year, after two guys had had their way with her on a group trip to Ferrugem Beach. Then I remembered Marta, the eldest sister of Gil, a guy I had dated for a few months back in the *Orangutan* era. Marta had two abortions just because she hadn't wanted kids, a decision that at the time had struck me as extravagant and a little immoral. In both cases, she had told me, the sperm purveyors had been in agreement. And yet, devastation had nonetheless ensued in the forms of, respectively, a break-up and a divorce. But Rita and Marta lived in Porto Alegre. If the statistics were accurate, nearly a third of the women I knew in São Paulo had terminated or would terminate a pregnancy.

Suddenly, I thought of someone who could help. I left my office, walked down the stairs, trembled with anger and fear past the gallons of highly flammable organic solvents still sitting in the facility's halls, turned left down the next corridor, walked to the end, and knocked on Vanessa Lieberknecht's office door. The Department of Biochemistry's most powerful faculty member, Vanessa was a tireless figure who, on top of leading cutting-edge research on redox processes, was one of only two women on the National Council for Scientific and Technological Development, which was otherwise composed of a group of sixteen men. What's more, rumor had it that as a young woman she'd written an RPG book that was pretty popular in its time, and that she and a group of friends still played together. When I'd first arrived at the university, I'd been a bit scared to approach her. About a year ago, though, we'd had a mojito-lubricated tête-à-tête at a karaoke bar in Liberdade during the post-dissertation defense party of one of her advisees. Vanessa and her husband, a researcher in Bioinformatics, had met in college and had two small children. At some point that night, we'd sung Raul Seixas's "A Maçã" on the karaoke machine. She'd been in her high school choir and I wasn't too shabby myself, and together we managed to raise applause from the audience. Back at the table, jokes about our singing skills moved the conversation toward work, and I asked how she had managed to balance it all so well with motherhood. As a hulk in a wife-beater and army pants sang Tears for Fears' "Woman in Chains" with shocking aplomb, she confessed that the truth was she hadn't and painted a picture that included quarterly marital crises and never enough time spent with her kids. She asked if I planned on having children, and I denied it with a firmness that rang false considering I was still on the fence about it then and even believed that the world could, sure, why not, be improved for future generations. In a surge of honesty, she had confided in me that she'd recently aborted the fetus that would have been her third child.

Vanessa wasn't in her office when I stopped by, so I sent her an email and she responded by scheduling a time for us to meet. She thought I wanted to discuss my second examination and assured me the committee would pass me; rumors about my previous failure had spread through the Institute of Chemistry and had reflected very poorly on César. It was comforting to hear this from a woman I admired so much. I could picture Vanessa being named rector someday. She, who could assert her views on the highest institutional echelons, on the same level with the men sitting at the Mount Olympus of academic politicking, all without totally losing her grace or levity. It was just as easy to picture her as the blond, curly-haired nerd who had graduated two decades ago. I had the urge to confess to her that I sometimes watched her from afar, with fascination, as she alternated again and again between Vulnerable Angel and Leader of the Pack, breaking into a toothy smile and then pursing her lips and going stiff from head to toe, seeming at once capable of lulling and eviscerating her interlocutors repeatedly in the space of a single conversation, be they fearful advisees or colleagues with whom she was arguing over budgets and resources. I mattered to her, that much was clear, but I knew our relationship was still one of goodwill rather than friendship.

I had to wait for the conversation to stagnate before I could admit the real reason for my visit. What followed was an extraordinarily strange moment in which she morphed into Leader of the Pack Vanessa and stared at me as if I'd crossed some forbidden line. After an awkward silence during which I considered apologizing and leaving, she altered her physiognomy completely, as if suddenly understanding that I wouldn't have come to her if I'd had anyone else to turn to on the matter. She then quickly embodied angelic Vanessa and asked me to explain my situation. In the end, she said she had paid five thousand reals for an abortion during her ninth week. She didn't have the clinic's contact details on hand but would look for them at home. A few days later, she sent me a note with the subject line "In the name of science" and a phone number in the body of the email. And now there I was, on Largo da Batata, describing zigzags through a herd of passersby, on my way to a residential street in the most middle-class section of the neighborhood.

I left the infestation of Largo da Batata, walked a few blocks along Rua dos Pinheiros, veered into a side street, and walked some more until I reached the one marked with a star on Google Maps. The building was a gray, gardenless town house, its entrance a small door embedded into the garage gate. I stood beneath the security camera and rang the intercom. Seconds later, the door opened. At nine thirty in the morning, they ran a blood test to confirm that I was pregnant. I went to kill time at the nearest bakery I could find. I had to fast, and kept hunger at bay by scrolling through Twitter and Facebook, now and then turning my attention to the television in the bakery, where Ana Maria Braga and Louro José were chatting with a juice detox specialist who subjected a series of fresh fruits to processes of liquefaction, and little by little I slipped into a state of consciousness similar to somnambulism.

At eleven, I walked back to the clinic. My seventh-week abortion would cost four thousand reals, and the doctor had an opening midafternoon. Once again on the street, I checked my bank statement with my cellphone app. After asking for directions at the corner kiosk, I walked to the nearest Banco do Brasil and made a withdrawal. I rambled, popping into shops that sold trinkets. At two fifteen, I went back to the clinic.

The doctor was a thin, balding man with a clean-shaven face and calm demeanor. Before pulling on his surgical mask, he told me only that I would be sedated—just a little prick—and that after I woke up, I might feel some pain and would have to remain under observation for an hour or two before being released. He shared no details about the procedure, but I knew that a tube would be inserted into my cervix and used to suction the fetus—or "material," as it was referred to in an anonymous online testimonial by a gynecologist who worked after hours at an abortion clinic. Just before I lay down on the stretcher, a shiver rose through my throat and was released as hot breath with a whiff of fermentation. It's always disconcerting to inhale your own breath and become aware of the scent wafting up from your recesses. There were certain ways the body had of imposing its presence that could mean only one thing: the existence of some emotional instability. Andrei had written in one of his books that depression was the body calling attention to itself, imposing itself, mastering the mind by fire and whip until it bent to its needs. My own fusty breath was the cracking of the whip, and my mind wanted to cower. But I had no doubts about what I wanted to do. My fear, in brief, was the garden-variety fear felt by anyone on the cusp of a medical intervention, an insurgent instinct against physical violence. The problem wasn't pain but rather the abrupt realization that I was absolutely alone, coupled with the anxiety I often felt when I was about to be touched someplace I usually wasn't or wouldn't allow myself to be touched, the sensitivity of internal cavities that mustn't ever be stimulated. They sedated me with injectable midazolam, the same anesthetic that in its oral form was known as "Goodnight Cinderella," a favorite of abusers and rapists. I savored the irony of this fact as the doctor asked me to count down from ten.

I woke up to caustic cramps and received pills for the pain. Two hours later I was on my way home in a cab, a drugstore bag with a packet of sanitary napkins in my lap. In the words of the chubby-cheeked girl who looked after me in the recovery room, light bleeding, "almost like menstruation," was normal in the first few days. In the absence of any "emotional turmoil," I could resume usual activities in two to three days. Night was falling. Through the taxi window, whose glass was covered in a dark film, São Paulo looked beautiful to me for the first time in ages, crosshatched in yellow, red, and green by the lights of vehicles and traffic signals, and bathed in a cavernous blue of uncertain origin. A beauty of artificial lights where, once the world ended, there would exist only pitch-darkness. Sitting in the comfort of the back seat, which seemed to guard me like a spaceship cabin from the hostile world outside, the vision of a baby with Antero's slant eyes popped into my head. I was expecting him, and calmly took him in. If I didn't welcome him in my thoughts, nowhere else would, either. Soothed, the baby gradually dissolved into the darkness of my mind, as if falling asleep. The turns in the road made my temple stick then come unstuck from the surface of the car window, which grew greasy with oil from my skin.

My weekend of recovery was a sort of delirious séance of painkillers, glasses of Ovomaltine and milk put through the blender, and sessions of reading articles and editing a PowerPoint presentation. I called my parents early Saturday morning. My mother answered and, maybe because I'd called at an unusual time or because my greeting had sounded slurred to her keen maternal ear, asked immediately if there was anything wrong. I said nothing was wrong, I'd just woken up, that was all. She was roasting croaker fish with potatoes for lunch. She said her shoulder hurt, that she suspected it was bursitis, then asked about my new doctoral defense and what I thought of the controversy surrounding Andrei's archives. I'd been following the "debate" on Facebook. Andrei's girlfriend, Francine, who reminded me a little of the French actor Louis Garrel, was leading a crusade to erase not only all of the unpublished material he had left behind but also all of his profiles and content from a variety of social media. Much as it had all seemed to indicate, Andrei's notorious rejection of social media—which he had removed himself from completely before his murder—was all false posturing for the handful of fake profiles he'd kept active on Facebook and Twitter, not to mention the countless profiles on dating apps and older or less popular social media networks. Francine told the press that Andrei had used them mostly as research for his fiction, though he'd kept some accounts for personal use. He'd also published pieces on a Tumblr account that one of his fans had chanced upon. *Folha de S. Paulo* had reprinted one of the texts on the last page of their literary supplement, *Ilustríssima*, generating a whole discussion around the rights situation in a piece that was still available online long after the death of the author responsible for said anonymous blog. Francine had in her possession some form of a will, signed and notarized by Andrei, in which he determined that, among other things, his unpublished writings, documents, chat logs, and online presence as a whole should, in the event of his death, be expunged. He had also left a list with his usernames and passwords in a sealed envelope. Francine was waging a personal war against editors, journalists, and websites that claimed they couldn't delete their content. Andrei's family had released a statement to the effect that their son had been very private about his work process and that they wanted only to respect the wishes he'd made in life. My mother agreed with Francine. I, on the other hand, thought that she'd concocted a fair amount of it herself just to get attention and that the fact that her position was based on Andrei's wishes and instructions didn't stop it from being idiotic. Andrei was dead. He had lived in the internet age, had gotten his hands dirty in it, and—with the stories and literary experiments he'd published in *Orangutan* and other digital publications across Brazil in the nineties—had helped "invent" the internet as a publishing platform. This crusade for his privacy struck me as a bunch of self-centered BS. My mom passed the phone to my dad, who, after successfully recovering from surgery, seemed to have channeled his vague indignation about the state of things into a feeling of festive opposition to PT, the Workers' Party.

"Did you hear that your dear guerrilla Dilma's been implicated in the Petrobrás racket?" he buzzed. "Bye-bye, reelection."

"All I know is she's been good to women researchers, Dad. Call me a PT hack all you want."

"Don't say that, sweetie. I've got a weak heart. You'll kill your pops with sorrow."

"I'm voting for her out of pure self-interest. I need the research grants. Ideologically, I'm an anarcho-capitalist."

"You can joke all you like, kiddo. Last time this country went through a crisis, you were too young to understand. Soon you'll see there's nothing funny about it at all."

At home, we barely ever discussed politics. On the few times the subject was raised, our conversation would turn into a careful game whose aim was to avoid any form of clear or radical positioning. It had always been easier to discuss sex than politics at my parents' dinner table. Though the former was more awkward, bordering on illicit, it at least managed to wrest from us firm and adult stances. The fact that we could openly discuss abortion and STDs during commercial breaks, ever since I was a teenager, had made us feel proud as a family, and it was because of this that I knew my parents were "pro-life," and that they knew I was "pro-life," too, and that we knew that to me and to them those words meant very different things and that equating the life of a zygote with that of an adult woman well-versed in feminism and biology could be complicated to say the least. The latter, politics, was a slipperier topic, but only in its more lighthearted and uncompromised modes, a step above meteorology in the world of small talk. Which is why my dad's abrupt transformation into a grotesque wingnut—the kind who interrupted a conversation with political provocations that were completely unrelated to the matter at hand—struck me as odd. It was almost as if his heart attack had left behind a subtle neurological sequela. Or maybe it was the somewhat sinister winds we sensed on the streets and in news programs.

For my part, the existential weariness I had been feeling since my last trip to Porto Alegre was still strong. A weariness that quashed any impulse toward indignation. Eight months ago, I'd marched with a group of college friends down avenues in São Paulo and let myself be swept up in the catharsis of the masses and their unpartisan war cries against the World Cup, corruption, and the bloody holes left on the backs, arms, and eyes of protesters by the police's rubber bullets. For a few days, there was the feeling that change might be possible. The bus fare hikes had been rescinded, and the government embarrassed itself by throwing us scraps of promises, heeding a claim here and there, and airing cringeworthy commercials in response to the pressure coming at them from the streets. Even this had given us some hope for the future. After the protests, though, as tens of thousands of people dispersed, I went looking for a cab amid empty beer cans and abandoned protest signs, from Avenida Brigadeiro Faria Lima halfway down Avenida Rebouças, my knees aching and calves stiff with lactic acid and, once home, was gripped by a sense of waste and futility. I was convinced nothing would change, that nothing *could* change.

What had stuck with me most from that phone call was my mom's reference to Andrei. It was like now that he was gone, he was close to me again, and he could support and understand me. It was all a bit absurd, keeping in mind that our friendship had petered out long before his death. I fantasized that he had faked his own death and was, right that second, monitoring the aftermath of his departure from an isolated cabin on the coast of Uruguay, cigarettes and papers laid out on a rustic table facing the ocean, along with half a dozen books and a laptop with satellite internet, writing a novel that he would then plant in some strategic place so that it would appear to be an original, posthumous work, one in which his death and its aftereffects were foreshadowed with hair-raising precision. It was the kind of thing Andrei was capable of.

I'm not sure why I thought of the time we left a party together—drunk and angry at life, each for our own reasons—and he suggested we drive to Cidreira to watch the sun rise over the ocean. Back then, no one thought twice about driving drunk; there were no stings nor any notion at all of the risks involved, so we sped down to the beach at a hundred and twenty kilometers an hour, listening to PJ Harvey's first album on tape. He drove a gray Del Rey with cream-colored leather seats, a charming banger full of weird noises whose bottom seemed like it might drop out at any moment. Andrei liked to tell the story of how he'd bought the car off a cattle breeder on the border. First launched as a luxury model, it was now worth less than a low-cylinder motorcycle. That night in 1999 might have felt like the high point of my sense of youthfulness. Andrei, Antero, our college and e-zine friends, and I used to all joke that 1999 would be a year like no other, not knowing that we were right. We talked in the car until the sun warmed our chests through the windshield, assuring ourselves that the world's ignorance—and our sexual and emotional frustrations—wouldn't get in the way of our glorious paths, that we were the best at what we liked doing and would be recognized for it. At some point, I rested my head on his shoulder. I think that was the only time I ever thought of sleeping with him. Nothing happened. I was sure that seafront aurora would make it into one of his books, and it had.

One of Andrei's favorite books was *The Myth of Sisyphus*. During the semester we'd been classmates in Communications Studies at the Federal University of Rio Grande do Sul, before I transferred to Biology, he'd declared to me that every philosophical dilemma sooner or later went back to Camus's reflections in that book. If we lost faith in our *tenacity* to push that rock up that mountain again and again—even though divine punishment had determined it would always roll back down to the foot of the mountain—there'd come a time when we'd be left with nothing, absolutely nothing. Thinking of this, I twisted and turned in bed, clutching my legs and clenching my abs. From time to time my suctioned uterus regained consciousness and yelped like a dog recovering from surgery planted in the middle of the room with an Elizabethan collar fastened around its neck. I opened my laptop, saved and closed the PowerPoint document, and, without much thought to what I was doing, wrote a letter, one I would have sent to Andrei had he still been alive. In it, I essentially told him that Sisyphus was lucky to have lived in ancient times. Were he alive now, he'd know too much about the rock, the mountain, and himself to surrender eternally to the absurdity of his task. He would know too much about the task itself. He would have science and technology. The history of the last two thousand years and the cloud of information. An overpopulation of Sisyphuses, a multiverse of Sisyphuses. Were he a product of our time, Sisyphus would have read *The Myth of Sisyphus*. He would've reached a point when he no longer understood a thing, not even the freedom he could find in his punishment. What would he think if his absurd heroism were to manifest as colorful clouds in brain MRI scans taken in neuroscience labs? What would remain of his rebellion amid such considerations as caloric expenditure and evolutionary explanations for the moral judgments of humankind? He wouldn't even be able to believe in gods. Not even obedience would remain. Only captivity and the sameness of his task.

I published my letter to Andrei on my Facebook page. It was soon buried in the torrents of posts about him flooding the internet since the day he died. There were so many more than anyone could have predicted, and they didn't stop, just kept coming. I thought that, if he were alive someplace, secretly tracking the aftereffects of his own death, he would definitely have come across my piece. Maybe he'd send me some sign of acknowledgment. A GIF of Sisyphus rolling his rock. A winking-eye emoji.

It was Emiliano, though, who reached out to me that evening, about two hours after I posted the letter. We'd exchanged phone numbers that night at Sabor Um after Andrei's funeral. He texted me "Hey" on WhatsApp, asked if

I could talk, and I told him to call—I wanted to talk to someone for real.

"Everything all right?" he asked as soon as we'd finished saying hello. It was the strangest thing in the world, but just the sound of his voice brought me an enormous sense of relief. Like getting a phone call from an older brother I hadn't spoken to in years. An older brother for whom I nurtured a nebulous sexual attraction, a fascination that, though inoffensive in practice, never went away, precisely because of its incestuous nature. Emiliano may not have been my brother, but he was gay, and if that didn't raise some sort of barrier, it was enough to lend my feelings an air of transgression. At times, the ideal alignment of all these factors had resulted in a desire as unexpected as it had been intensely concrete, and which I satiated by scrolling through photos of him online. In them, Emiliano seemed proud of the hard-hat physique that he maintained with exercise, a figure that clashed with the bags under his eyes and eyelids swollen with beer, cigarettes, and the insomnia that he'd both brag and gripe about in a single breath. He was one of those guys who kept in good shape so he wouldn't have to forgo his vices. It was a combo I liked. But I was invisible to him.

"I saw your letter to Andrei," Emiliano said, right after I lied and said everything was fine. "It reminds me a little of the pieces you used to write for *Orangutan* back in the day. It's really great, but I also think it might be a symptom of . . ."

He didn't finish.

"Depression?" I ventured.

"I was going to say loneliness. A lack of living people to talk to."

It was like I'd swallowed a fish bone and had to decide whether to shove my finger down my throat or let it pass.

"I've always been a bit of a loner, though, haven't I? You remember that tattoo on my wrist?"

"Yeah, it's a series of letters."

"R, T, E, S. It's an acronym. Remember to enjoy solitude."

"I don't think you ever told me what it meant."

"I never told anyone."

"Is it from a song?"

"No, it's just something I used to tell myself all the time as a kid. A reminder. Sometimes, I used to catch myself hurting when I was alone and then I'd remember how much I hurt the rest of the time, for wanting to be alone. These days, I don't need to remind myself so much anymore, but the tattoo is a way of remembering that this used to be the case, it's good. But I'm all right. I'm glad you called. I wrote that piece thinking Andrei might be alive somewhere, surfing the web, monitoring the effect his death had on people. I decided to post it as a joke, sort of. He hasn't reached out to you, has he?"

Emiliano laughed.

"I'm not supposed to say anything, but the truth is he's at my parents' ranch. He faked his own death with help from friends in high places and decided to spend the rest of his days growing watermelons."

"That ranch where we spent the turn of the millennium?"

"That's the one."

Almost fifteen years had passed, and I could still remember the palmettos I never saw anywhere else, the guans and seriemas that we glimpsed in the shadows of the dirt road, the bothrop Antero found under a rock and Emiliano killed with a huge stick, swimming in the muddy reservoirs and shitting in the bush, the stuffy tent I slept in with my boyfriend of the time, a newborn foal, old graveyards concealed by the growth, the silence and isolation that seemed to keep that corner of the world out of the reach of civilization and the cataclysms that might one day destroy it.

"I'm just kidding, Aurora. Obviously," Emiliano said, taking my silence as I accessed the memory as the absence of a response, caused by a literal interpretation of what he'd just said.

"I know. I was just thinking about the ranch. Is it still there?"

"Yeah. I never went back, but my parents go there from time to time. It's pretty abandoned. The vegetation is overgrown, and I think there are a few goats running amok. Then again, we've had electricity and a bathroom for a few years now."

"It'd be cool to go back sometime."

"We could do that. Something else for us to discuss later.

I haven't told you why I called. Here goes. I'm writing something about Andrei, and I wanted to talk to you. To interview you."

"Writing what, a profile?"

"A text."

"Like, a magazine article?"

"A biography."

"*Andrei's* biography?"

"I know what you're thinking. That it's too soon. That Andrei would never have wanted it."

"That's not quite what I'm thinking. I'm not sure what I'm thinking. It's just that—"

He sighed on the other end of the phone line. I heard the lid of his famed Jack Daniel's Zippo click open.

"Somebody's going to write it, Aurora, sooner rather than later. That's what the person who convinced me to accept the assignment told me. There are loads of guys itching to do it. I can write a book that does him justice."

"Don't you find it disturbing to write a biography of someone you were so close to?"

"We were never close. We hadn't spoken in years."

"You know what I mean, Êmi. We were all part of the same friend group. It's weird for someone *on the inside* to do that, you know? Also, all this talk of a biography sort of kills him all at once, or all over again. I don't think I've come to terms with his death yet."

"I wanted to talk to you about it in person. I'd love it if

we could meet in São Paulo. In about ten days. I'll be up there for a week doing interviews."

Emiliano was right. Someone would write it. And, the more I thought about it, the harder it became not to suspect Duke would have *wanted* to be the subject of some form of posthumous research, even if he had conspired to erase his digital tracks. Verses of the same song. I pictured him again in his hiding place, basking in the aftermath of his own death.

"Remember how Andrei would sometimes say that Andy Kaufman was still alive? That he'd probably resurface decades later and deliver the punch line to the greatest joke of all time?"

"Huh? No, I don't remember. What does that have to do with anything?"

"Nothing, I'm just thinking out loud. Of course we can talk about him, Êmi. It just has to be after my defense, on April 4. I won't manage to do anything else properly until then."

"All right, the fourth is a Friday, we can meet that weekend or the following week. I'll extend my stay if I have to. What defense?"

"The new doctoral defense. I failed the first one, remember? I mentioned it at Sabor Um."

"That's right. The circadian rhythm of plants. You got screwed by a professor on the committee, was that it?"

That was the gist of it, but how could I explain the whole

story to him, a story that went beyond my quarrel with César and my subsequent failure and encompassed the entire past decade of my life? César Moreira was one of the bioenergy bigwigs of the Biochemistry Institute, and the postgraduate program had selected him to sit on the evaluating committee for my defense. César had always struck me as friendly, though his breath stank to high hell. He was always nice to me whenever he passed me in the Institute's corridors, and once, when my freezer had broken, he let me store sugarcane samples and RNA in his freezer while a repair was arranged for mine. I idolized him a little, as I often did anyone who had devoted their life to science or academia. Thinking of him, the adjective that came to mind was "solid." My impression was that, given the opportunity to get to know him better, I'd discover that he had done some other incredible thing that was completely unrelated to academia, like running an ultramarathon or winning an international culinary competition.

A few days after the committee was finalized, I went for lunch on my own at one of the university restaurants near the Chemistry Department. I had to get home to let a plumber in to fix the toilet flushing mechanism, so I was scarfing down my food, when César asked to sit at my table. Though I was surprised to see him, the restaurant was packed and he would have to share a table with someone, so it hadn't struck me as particularly suspect. Even though César couldn't be older than fifty, his voice was like that of a kindly grandpa in one of those commercials aired by multinationals around Christmastime. By the time I had to leave to catch the bus, César had barely taken a bite. The next day he sent me an email in which he regretted that I'd had to leave so quickly and suggested we schedule a coffee date to talk. Now, that had seemed suspect, highly suspect. Professors like César didn't mix with plebs like me. When I mentioned this to Matias, another advisee in my lab, he said—in a sincere attempt at a joke—that they'd definitely pass me if I wore a minidress to my defense. Maybe I could have told Emiliano about the time, years earlier, when I had gotten my period in the middle of a postgrad exam, an inconvenience with the potential for calamity seeing as I was wearing a white skirt. I had gone up to the professor, explained the situation, and asked to go to the bathroom. Understanding and compassionate, he had given me permission. Two days later, the results were published, and I saw that I had gotten a C, even though I'd given the exact same responses as the student whose exam they used as an example of the highest grade. When I went to have words with the department head, I discovered the professor had accused me of going to the bathroom to cheat, which besides being untrue was also a ridiculous insinuation in a postgraduate setting. Too embarrassed to confront him, that blemish had remained on my CV, a reminder that I would have to work harder than any man to achieve the same results.

What I hadn't fathomed, as Matias cracked his little

joke, was that he might be right. The day after I handed in my presentation summary to the committee, César once again intercepted me in the corridor. Briefly, we discussed *Game of Thrones* and a recently published article on the cutting-edge CRISPR/Cas9 gene-editing system, which quickly dispelled my suspicions and unease. Then, César abruptly declared that he had come across some unexpected shortfalls in my abstract and felt that certain experiments hadn't been adequate, a fact that greatly surprised him. It was inappropriate of him to say. He shouldn't have raised the issue with me at all. And then he added something or other about the importance of being resourceful in academia, of knowing how to interact with people. Shocked, I continued to quietly nod my head. Though exceedingly subtle, his message was unequivocal. After glancing to either side and squeezing my shoulder with his hand, César said goodbye and left me standing alone in the corridor.

It would have been almost impossible to change the date of the defense or find a replacement juror. There were no substitutes available for that specific day. I could have tried to make Emiliano understand how my frustration had slowly turned to rage, and my doubts about how I'd read the situation turned into a feeling of powerlessness, but even so, it would have been hard to explain why I'd gone up to César on another afternoon, days after the shoulder-squeeze incident in the corridor, and suggested he put out his cigarette. I'd been walking down the ground-floor hallway, a polystyrene case of dry ice in my arms, when I'd spotted César chatting to a man right next to the stacks of blue plastic drums filled with organic solvent, smoking his cigarette as if beside him, just two meters from where he stood, there wasn't enough flammable material to blow up the entire Institute of Chemistry. Regardless, smoking was forbidden throughout the building, a regulation César had routinely disregarded, as if his Lattes profile brimming with published articles exempted him from all health and safety regulations. But this time, he'd gone too far. I'd already filed a complaint with management about those neglected, irregularly stored drums and had heard in response that a bureaucratic process had delayed their contracting the company responsible for collecting and discarding those solvents. Nobody but me seemed to care. These two sources of exasperation fused diabolically in the scene before me, and I lost control. Next thing I knew, I was interrupting their conversation and saying, in the sweetest voice I could muster, that smoking was forbidden in that area, especially right next to *those*. I pointed to the stack of plastic drums and frowned. I never knew who it was César had been speaking to then, but he must have been important, because César began to shake, and several seconds passed before he managed to stutter that, though he appreciated the consideration, he would smoke wherever he well pleased. Then I said I had no other recourse but to file a complaint with management, which I hadn't the least intention of doing. César responded that he'd eagerly await the arrival of said notice, and after a brief, perplexed look—as if he couldn't quite believe he'd just had this exchange with a doctoral candidate—resumed his conversation with the man. I'd already turned my back to them and was walking away, feeling the penny drop on what I had just set in motion, when again I heard César's meek voice.

"Jane Henderson."

I stopped but didn't turn around.

"*Paris, Texas*, right? Great film."

I turned around then, but César was no longer looking at me, if he had been before. He was talking to the man again. My body wobbled so much I was scared I'd drop the case of dry ice. I forgot all about the material I was planning to collect from my freezer and walked back to my lab. Jane Henderson was the name of Nastassja Kinski's character in a Wim Wenders film, but janehendersonlove was my handle on Chaturbate, where I exposed myself via my laptop camera once or twice a month. It was possible César frequented that site often enough to have randomly stumbled into my chatroom, but it was far more probable that one of his students had recognized me and tipped him off to it, along with who knows how many others. I'd never know. My chatroom on Chaturbate didn't quite fit the prevalent archetype of explicit sex that most users seemed interested in. When, out of curiosity, I had accessed the site for the first time, on the hunt for something exciting and unexpected,

I'd felt discouraged by the prevalent tips-for-titties dynamic in most chatrooms. What I had pictured as a transgressive world of exhibitionism had revealed itself to be, at first glance, a gallery of uninspiring peep shows aping the clichés of male-targeted pornography. Young women humming hip-hop tunes with artificial smiles, robotically thanking users for their tips only to immediately flash their tits or turn over onto all fours and slip vibrators into their pussies, all for the exact two minutes promised on the menu of performative acts listed in their profiles, while in the chatrooms men behaved like men, letting girls know that if they'd been their little sisters, they'd have snuck into their rooms at night, or that they wanted to cum in their faces. Even so, on lonely nights in the months when I worked so late I didn't have the energy to set up any live dates with the few men who interested me on Facebook, or with those in the realm of real-life relationships, I'd log on to Chaturbate, because there was something there, in the less popular chatrooms, the ones harder to find, that I identified with. With time, I found the people who seemed to be there just because they wanted to, dancing by themselves in Gothic-styled rooms or sitting listlessly on unkempt beds wearing S&M get-ups as if they were pajamas, their faces at times partially offscreen or concealed behind animals masks, doing nothing but receiving torrents of praise for their large, natural breasts while listening to classical music, toying with extravagant vibrators, or discussing Murakami's novels, showing strangers a little of their bodies and of their eccentricities, not in exchange for tips but because it was exciting or because it gave them a sense of control and power, since they, the people on show, were the ones who created their audience and dictated the rules, attracting or banning at will the people with whom they interacted, sheltered by the physical distance.

Or at least that's what I felt when, in a bra and panties, I turned my camera on for the first time and waited to see what would happen. In a matter of seconds, a guy told me to show him my pussy, and I banned him. Then I sat there a while longer, chatting with users who seemed to display some form of human interest that was neither needy nor authoritarian, and after an hour or so, I ended up undressing and fulfilling certain requests that I received via chat, showing my feet, my butt, touching myself according to certain specific instructions, and I liked it so much that I had to turn off the camera so I could finish masturbating and bring myself to climax, which I wasn't comfortable doing live that first time. What bothered me when I reached that point was that I couldn't see the people who could see me. I craved reciprocity. With time, I discovered that it was easy to set up dates in private, password-restricted chatrooms with guys who leaned back in their chairs in front of their computers, cocks hard, lit only by the light from the computer screen, waiting for the Chaturbate lottery to bestow them a girl somewhere on the planet who was willing to partake in a virtual fuck. So, this is how it went, me exposing myself a bit to get warmed up, and then finding someone for a private chat. Sometimes with couples, or duos of men, or even trios. With some, I felt confident enough to Skype and struck up virtual friendships in a manner reminiscent of the late-nineties naïveté of ICQ and the first UOL chatrooms, back when there still existed a sense of allure and discovery at the mere possibility of trading messages about the weather or favorite books with some guy in Sergipe, Brazil, or St. Petersburg, Russia, while making innuendos and polite sexual overtures; the feeling of corrupting known rules of social engagement and experiencing human contact with no known consequences or responsibilities, or at least with other consequences and responsibilities that were new and not always clear. There was a forty-or-so-year-old American couple who liked to watch me while they fucked, and another American with a hairy chest and small, babyish eyes, whose belly hair always looked recently brushed, with whom I masturbated simultaneously, and a Uruguayan publicist who looked more like an underwear model who sometimes asked me to wrap my head in a black shirt and one day introduced me to his Kenyan girlfriend, who was waiting to apply for citizenship, a beautiful woman in a white silk dress who didn't like to take part in the sessions but would say a friendly hello and goodbye and walk past in the background while we chatted. I always knew there was some risk in exposing myself, and this was part of the attraction, but now I had to deal with the possibility that one of the men who had called me hot in the chat box as I sipped at my drink with my tits hanging out at two in the morning, one of the men who sent me—using the site's virtual currency—tips I had never even asked for and that in all those months had never amounted to more than a handful of cash, or one of the men who just spied on me for a bit, without interacting with me in any way, one of them had been César, who in a few days would be sitting on the committee of my dissertation defense.

On the day of the defense, I could have continued explaining to Emiliano, César had greeted me effusively at the entrance to the room, as if we weren't both aware that he was about to screw me. He was wearing one of his loose-fitting, thick cotton T-shirts—this one a burnt beige—cut in a late-eighties style that made him look like a former communist activist on his way to a safari, or something like that. For two hours, I detailed the progress of my research to the committee. My goal was to better understand the mechanisms of the central oscillator of sugarcane's biological clock. One of the things that had most fascinated me while studying biology had been the relationship between living organisms and time. Living organisms could perceive time and the changes it entailed. Light, dark, winter, summer. This perception was then processed by the living organism's internal clock, which in turn generated physiological responses or metabolic rhythms. What most influenced the internal clocks was the cycle of days and nights, though some research on marine invertebrates had shown that certain organisms possessed multiple internal clocks that were synchronized to lunar phases, to the movement of tides, and other natural cycles. The human body knew how to control cell division, bone growth, sleep and wakefulness, as well as hormones and hunger, according to habits, based on the cycle of night and day. What had fascinated me during my undergraduate studies was how this might work on a molecular or cellular level, which was also why I decided to center my research on plants rather than animals. It had all started with the insight that plant lives were also regulated by their own internal clocks and no doubt also experienced time in some way. By conducting research on these organisms, I could also eschew the enormous range of ethical restrictions that were part and parcel of animal experimentation.

Years after observing my mother's jasmine tree in the backyard of our house, wondering how it knew when it was night or day so that it could release its delicious and pungent fragrance, always at the same hour, there I was collecting sugarcane leaves and internodes to extract RNA and analyze their gene expression, searching for rhythmicity. Among the physiological processes regulated by sugarcane's biological clock were growth and photosynthesis. If I obtained the results I hoped for, my research could have game-changing implications for the cultivation of that and other plants exploited for food and as energy sources, with a huge economic and environmental impact. Synthetic fertilizers and genetic engineering had furthered the Green Revolution and given us the ability to feed nearly seven billion people, but how would we feed the ten billion projected for the end of the twenty-first century? Fertilizers relied on fossil fuels, which generated a whole other set of environmental problems, and genetic modification was up against negative public opinion. Optimizing plant growth by means of their biological clock could be the innovation we needed to feed humanity for another few decades or even centuries. On my better days, when we obtained the results predicted and my adviser was in a good mood, I would let myself daydream of a cover story on *Science* magazine.

But not that afternoon, when, following positive remarks from the two other committee members, César had deemed the data collected to be insufficient, which was all rather discouraging, in his view, seeing as I'd been working on that project for two years. It was true, I'd come across some unforeseen snags in my research and had been forced to zigzag at certain points, yet I'd gathered the highest possible quantity of data and my main experiment had required fourteen months of work and analysis. Certain experiments still needed validating, and I now had a new hypothesis, arisen mid-research, which posited that sucrose was the synchronizing molecule of the SCLHY gene expression, a gene extremely responsive to the dark/light transition, and therefore capable of providing evidence of the perception and responsiveness of the internal clock to light. Many of the results had to be consolidated, and certain inadequacies were due to the nature of the research method. Any sensible committee would have taken this into account when evaluating my project, as had been the case with the two other professors, but César went from criticizing the insufficient data to claiming he would like to see new statistical analyses of the data already obtained, requesting technical reproductions of certain experiments, and even questioning the reliability of some results, demanding new validation by means of different techniques. None of it was really necessary, everyone there knew that, but he had the prerogative and the authority to fail me, which is exactly what he did. During the following days, as I spoke with my adviser, other professors, and doctoral colleagues, I realized everyone had known that this would happen, that my spat with César in the hallway had passed from mouth to mouth and reached everyone's ears—from the janitorial staff to the board of directors—even though I was pretty certain there had been no other witness besides the man César had been speaking to. Everyone was on my side, they said, but nothing could or would be done about it, and for weeks I was content to be on the receiving end of pity from the entire Institute of Chemistry, *that woman, the one who failed her dissertation defense*, which was akin to a leper lugging herself through a medieval village, and it was under those circumstances that I got a phone call from my mom informing me that my dad was in the middle of a surgical bypass.

*You got screwed by a professor on the committee, is that it?* Even if I decided to share the entire story with Emiliano, where did it begin and where would it end? Should it not also include Andrei's death in a robbery, the night I spent with Antero, yesterday afternoon's abortion, global warming, and the need to feed ten billion people with a new Green Revolution that didn't rely on fossil fuels?

"Yeah, a professor screwed me. There's a way out, though. I need to reorganize the data, add a few things here and there. The next committee will pass me."

"This guy's gonna hear some hard truths in your Nobel speech."

"I'll set him straight well before then."

"That's right. Sit on his face."

"Êmi!"

"Sorry, sometimes my delicate sensibilities refuse to be contained. So, here's what we're going to do. I'll call when I get to São Paulo, and we'll meet after the fourth. We can go get some moussaka at Acrópole."

"You're paying."

"My publisher's paying."

"Done."

After the phone call, I returned to my research. There was nothing much to do—it was all just for show—but I went through the motions of adding a few charts. I drew up a nifty one that illustrated the correlation between the normalized expression of certain genes in the +1 leaves of four-month-old plants and nine-month-old plants at specific times of day, according to light. It was a beauty, but, as soon as I added it to the Word document, I felt a sharp cramp and had to run to the bathroom to change my bloodied pad and take an anti-inflammatory pill I had neglected to take earlier. It was getting dark, and the wind shook the windows' tin frames, presaging a storm. My body begged for sleep, but my head was processing information uncontrolledly, like a computer only partially aware of its capabilities testing the limits of what it could do. A dash of Smirnoff and homemade limoncello would have done the trick, but I couldn't drink on medication. As always, the cause of my anxiety seemed within reach and yet wasn't to be found among the more obvious causes. It was hidden, somewhere close by, like a person standing behind me covering my eyes and asking, "Who is it?" Memories of research trips to collect samples from sugarcane fields circled my head like TV reruns. Sabrina, Matias, my adviser Clóvis, and me at a small hotel in Araras taking turns chopping down sugarcane plants every two hours, in teams of two, over a period of twenty-six hours, subjected to a sleep schedule that ended up throwing a wrench into our own circadian rhythms. After using a machete to cut down a sugarcane plant, we had to separate the first leaf with its own sheaf, the so-called +1 leaf, and then peel off the stem until we reached the draining tissue, the fifth internode in particular, which was then sliced and packaged in liquid nitrogen for lab analysis. A gaggle of nerds in black galoshes and white aprons filthy with red mud, delirious from lack of sleep but deep in concentration when it came to prepping and packaging the collected material, on their breaks chatting about TV shows and whether all grains and cereals belonged to the Poaceae family, without ever reaching a consensus. At night, we would gaze up at stars absent from São Paulo's skies. By day's end, a solemn circumspection would take hold of us, a mixture of exhaustion and prolonged dedication to such repetitive work. The sun had left us red and sunburned, suspicious as we were of the titanium dioxide in sunscreen and aware of the studies that claimed oxybenzone, the ingredient that absorbed ultraviolet rays, ended up in the oceans and corrupted coral DNA, that just a drop of sunblock in five Olympic-size pools was enough to discolor them and tamper with their normal growth patterns. None of us wanted to be party to that, did we? We drank instant coffee and ate instant noodles and supermarket-bought sandwiches in the research center's deserted cafeteria, thinking of the work that lay ahead of us and listening to the generators thrumming outside. Sabrina, who was always on a variety of diets, talked nonstop about cellular oxidation, nutrients, and energy input to the brain. To decompress, we would fashion dry ice bombs from PET bottles of sparkling water, laughing at the explosions like children in gated communities. The stray dogs of the University of São Carlos campus watched us from afar and, suspicious of our behavior, escorted us across the fields, our machetes and light meters in hand.

On those research trips, it was even easier to love what I did. The center's plantation contained dozens of sugarcane species at various stages of genetic advancement. Plants that promised faster growth, required less synthetic fertilizer and fewer agrotoxins, fed more people, generated more biofuel, and thrived in more diverse climates and soils. And that, I suddenly realized, was the crux of my anxiety. Science was the carburetor of our world, which was ever faster, teeming with people who lived longer and longer and every day consumed more and more than an industry also bolstered by science could produce, and the ideology behind all of these things was profit, sure, but also life, *more and more life*, when what I'd been feeling ever since my trip to Porto Alegre was just the opposite, a gut conviction that we'd long since passed the point of no return, that scientific and technological miracles—if they ever arrived, since there was no guarantee—would only press down harder on the accelerator, generating more consumption, more people, *more life*.

Humans weren't the first living organisms to create the conditions for their own genocide from an excess of evolutionary advantage—not even in that respect were we special. Agitated, I got out of bed, the cold porcelain tiles of the living room and hallway sticking to the soles of my feet. I walked to the window and breathed in the scent that the first bursts of rain expelled from São Paulo's sweltering asphalt—a smell that reminded me, weirdly, of the feces of some large creature—and I screamed, "Less life!" at the top of my lungs, about three or four times, like an idiot. But it helped. I went back to bed, feeling better, and in a matter of seconds was fast asleep.

A few days later, my second dissertation defense went on without incident. I passed and kept my doctoral grant. My parents called to ask about the result, as did Emiliano. As soon as I took leave from the professors on the evaluation committee, Vanessa intercepted me in the hallway and asked how everything had gone. I started to summarize what the committee had said, but she seemed baffled and interrupted.

"You had your defense today? I thought it was scheduled for next week."

"It was just now."

"Congratulations! I knew you'd ace it. But I was asking about the other thing."

I told her that everything had gone well and thanked her again for passing along the contact details. I may have come off seeming dumb. But those days, almost nothing mattered to me. The convictions I'd always held as a scientist, and as a biologist in particular, were being continually shaken, not by other ideas but by fear and anxiety. I was beginning to suspect that the world was neither ending nor advancing. It was static. It'd probably continue to stagnate, forever frozen in a state of perishing. Whenever I had this thought, the rage, fear, and anxiety that usually moved me to action gave way to a passivity that was nonetheless pleasant, compared to everything else.

There were dozens of passwords. All jotted down on a piece of paper kept in a sealed envelope. His girlfriend was to open the envelope in the event of his death. Duke's passwords, Francine told me, were extremely difficult to work out. He chose them by forming acronyms from the opening sentences of short stories or novels. I thought it was strange for Francine to refer to herself as Duke's girlfriend and not as his wife, or partner, or something that carried more weight. They'd been together for five years. It was clear that he had trusted her more than his own family. After entering the apartment and greeting her, I asked how she'd been coping with her loss. She said that she tried to stay as still as possible, to see if *all of that* would pass quickly. Francine spoke slowly, her voice that of a teenager on sedatives. She didn't seem downcast but instead resigned to mourning and to the role expected of her after her partner's passing. At the first instance of mutual hesitation, she took out her iPhone and started reading messages and texting with robotic diligence. The corners of her jaw pulsed. About a minute later, she put her phone on silent, left it on the nearest side table, and with her eyes expressed that from that moment on I'd have her complete attention.

The suspicion that I had first had at the funeral—that Duke had left Francine instructions that were to be observed in the event of his death—was not only confirmed but surpassed my speculations. The precautions taken for his posterity betrayed an unthinkable degree of obsession and paranoia. Or, who knows, maybe an excess of imagination. Francine wouldn't show me the letter but confirmed it contained instructions to the effect that all drafts, proofs, unpublished works, and notes were to be destroyed, along with any of the deceased's digital footprints. There were also guidelines about what to do with his belongings and investments, suggestions for the funeral and all kinds of other practical matters. He had updated the informal will contained in the envelope a few times. There were four addendums in total. On average, one per year.

Francine had already deleted nearly all of Duke's email accounts and online profiles, including some he had forgotten to list in his letter. For example, his PlayStation Network profile. According to Francine, after buying a PlayStation 3, Duke had spent a month and a half hooked on an RPG game called Skyrim. He'd play it for at least six hours a day, every day, until, grumbling that he couldn't get anything done anymore, he placed the console back in its box and never touched it again. Francine had also encountered certain difficulties in her quest to obliterate Andrei Dukelsky's online existence. Passwords were missing, and at times the website in question didn't offer any clear steps for the account's deletion. These were exceptions of little consequence, such as a username on a ticketing website or an old blog containing a handful of posts on an aborted literary project. She opened the page for the latter on her MacBook and turned the screen to me. In the space of half a dozen posts, Duke outlined his intention to write a novel that would narrate the history of the universe after the total extinction of life on Earth. I laughed, which left an aftertaste of melancholy in my mouth. It was so Duke. Francine looked at me as if suddenly realizing I was drunk. True, I was a bit drunk. Francine wore men's cologne. I didn't know what kind, except that it was for men. Though my tongue had the discernment of a doormat, I'd always had a keen nose. Hints of tangerine and pine. Her shirt looked like it was made of oakum. Her skirt resembled pants, or vice versa.

Francine reacted better than I had expected to the news that I'd been commissioned to write Duke's biography. That I was being paid to do it. Like Frank, she felt a biography was inevitable, and that the project might as well fall to someone who had loved and respected him. I decided not to ask why she thought I'd loved Duke. I had. But what did she know? In that instant, the implications of the work I'd be doing hit me in full. I would have the opportunity to find out more about what Duke had thought of me. His version of those things that I remembered in my own way. The prospect of stirring up the muck at the bottom of that river wasn't the least bit appealing to me. Just then, I couldn't help myself and asked if I could light my first cigarette, pre-emptively getting up and motioning toward the living room window. Francine said it wasn't necessary and signaled at the sooty ashtray on the coffee table. Beneath the window was a ledge with half a dozen maidenhair ferns in small planters. I knew they were maidenhair ferns because Duke was always describing them in his books. They adorned several of his characters' homes. He loved those ferns. They were difficult to care for, Francine said. Duke and Francine's ferns were full of life, green and delicate in the warm light that fell into their rear apartment. If I touched them, I thought, they would disintegrate.

My face was greasy from the humidity in the air. Temperatures had fallen after the hottest summer in decades, but the humidity hadn't eased up. The soot from the bus terminal at Porto Alegre's Public Market, where I had lunch before meeting Francine, reeked in my hair. My briefs were clammy with sweat, and I could swear a stench of swamp crotch wafted up from between my legs. Despite all this, Francine watched me with a curiosity that, little by little, began to seem like more than mere curiosity. A look I could only define as *willingness*. She was *willing*. Under those circumstances, which included Duke's still-fresh death and our somewhat tense conversation about the biography, her gaze made me realize that she was a woman *willing to do absolutely anything*.

Once she'd agreed, with a resigned and pragmatic sigh, to the idea of a biography, Francine explained that the limits of her collaboration would be in line with Andrei's wishes, per his will and the things they'd always agreed should remain private. It all seemed reasonable to me, I said. She gave me access to his bookcases, which held approximately fifteen hundred volumes and would be donated to whatever library guaranteed them the best fate. I photographed the shelves with her permission. Those book spines might very well tell a story. We left his office and returned to the living room.

This was followed by nearly two hours during which Francine didn't respond to a single question. She didn't talk about Duke's habits. Nor about what she knew of his work process. Nor how they'd met, the ins and outs of their relationship. She didn't want to discuss Duke's family nor disclose his favorite color. She preferred to abstain in matters of the deceased author's tastes in television shows and regional cuisine; his relationship with critics and the press; the dreams and frustrations he'd aired out in private. It took me about fifteen minutes to understand the game we were playing. I decided to follow it through to the end, asking every question that popped into my head, until we were exhausted or had reached some sort of impasse. We were nearing exhaustion, at least I was, when I asked her about

Andrei's sexual preferences. For the first time during that interview, Francine offered me some form of response.

"He liked girls that looked a bit like men."

"Meaning young girls?"

"No. Girls in the general sense of the term. Women."

"And what do you like?" I asked, realizing the situation was no longer in my control. As the words left my mouth, I noticed that my question echoed the one Duke had asked me the night we met.

"Confused men."

I checked the time on my cellphone. I felt disoriented and knew that soon I would say or do something stupid. Could she be playing games with me? Whatever it was, in that moment I forgot Duke for the first time and realized I knew very little about Francine. She was the most important piece in the story I was going to write. By asking her about herself, certain things about Duke might come to light, too. I knew Francine wouldn't give satisfactory responses to any pertinent questions. There was a strategy for this kind of situation. Impertinent questions.

"How much do you weigh, Francine?"

She pulled a face, and an involuntary response left her lips.

"Fifty-one kilos."

The next step was to preserve said impertinence with a question completely unrelated to the previous one.

"Do you know who you'll be voting for this year?"

"I don't. What does that have to do with anything?"

"Nothing. I was just thinking, that's all. I'd like to know your thoughts on euthanasia, if that's not too sensitive an issue."

I knew I couldn't go this route much longer. Francine was far more intelligent than I was, and yet she smiled, baring her pointed canine teeth. Once the stick that had seemed permanently stuck up her ass had been removed, her beauty appeared even more vulgar and easier to digest. In twenty minutes, surgically alternating between seriousness and banter, I managed to pry a few bits of information from her. She was twenty-eight. She believed in God. She had contracted rhabdomyolysis at nineteen from an antidepressant and almost died. In the hospital, she'd learned that people shouldn't waste time on trivial problems. Her family was rich and from Caxias do Sul. Dad owned various businesses, including a pre-made housing factory and a distributor of flowers and decorative plants. Mom was a socialite. She had studied nutrition at IPA, quit halfway through, and gotten a degree in Literature from the Federal University of Rio Grande do Sul. In 2012, while researching a book, she had spent a week living with a mystical community that was preparing for the end of the world per the Mayan calendar. She was interested in how they would react once they realized that the end of the world hadn't arrived. She never wrote the book and refused to explain why. She had done a few paid translations of works from Italian and English into

Portuguese. Duke had left her the apartment, but she intended to sell it and split the proceeds with his parents. Spying her budding impatience, I decided to take a risk.

"Were you planning on having kids?"

"Me and Andrei?"

"Yes."

She propped her elbows on her knees and pinched her lips with her fingers. I thought she wouldn't respond.

"We were considering it. Andrei wanted to wait until 2016."

"Why?"

"Because he couldn't decide whether it was ethical to bring another person into the world."

"Can you think of why that year, specifically?"

She pouted somewhat pensively, then shook her head. Her eyes fogged up like windowpanes. I realized her mind was no longer there, with us. It had migrated to someplace in the past, or to some unspecified reality. This filled me with an inscrutable unease. I said, as softly as possible, that that was enough for now and I was ready to go. She got up and said she was always willing to help, I just had to call. She wished me luck with the biography.

"Before I forget—so you don't leave empty-handed—there's something I think Andrei would've liked you to have. He'd been researching a new novel for almost a year. He used to say that he had to hurry because every time he managed to see how the book would turn out, he realized it'd already become obsolete. Because of everything that had happened in the world in the meantime. It's just the book—"

She didn't complete her sentence. She gestured for me to wait and vanished down the hall. I heard drawers opening and sheets of paper being shuffled. When she returned, she was carrying a stack of printouts.

"This is his research for the novel. The draft is gone just like everything else, it was in a folder he wanted deleted and I deleted it. But I don't think he'd mind people seeing this. There are clippings, transcriptions from book passages, that sort of thing. It'll give you an idea of what he'd been interested in lately."

When she closed the door, I stood in the hallway for a few seconds, thinking I'd hear sobbing or swearing. But there was nothing.

Later, at home, a glass of Jim Beam with amaretto already in hand and a clean ashtray keeping me company in bed, I studied the contents of those two to three hundred sheets of paper. As Francine had predicted, they contained nothing resembling the draft of a novel. There were passages from essay collections, works of fiction and articles, as well as news clippings. All of it about the end of the world. Certain sections were underlined in pencil, and in some cases, there were notes in the margins. The works in question had titles such as *In Catastrophic Times*, *The Ends of the World*, *Hyperobjects: Philosophy, Ecology after the*

*End of the World*, and *Living in the End Times*. There was a stapled packet of anti-natalist quotes preaching that in an ideal scenario, we wouldn't be born at all. Schopenhauer, Cioran, a guy by the name of David Benatar. On the margins of the latter's citation, Duke had written, "In the end, moral imperative against suffering makes no sense; question of whether life is worth it is purely aesthetic." Generally, I couldn't make heads or tails of his notes. Many of them were about the concept of the Anthropocene, the new geological era that took its name from humankind's impact on the planet. Scientific articles on climate change and mass extinction, on the effects of the agricultural revolution and how carbon and radioactivity were altering the earth's atmosphere and crust. There was a piece called "Uncivilization—The Dark Mountain Manifesto," which preached that the only way to remedy the impending cataclysm that modernity had set in motion was to reverse the civilizing process. Another crammed with sheets of paper focused on things such as cyborgs, artificial intelligence, and Posthumanism. An article titled "Celestial Fetishism" criticized accelerationist fantasies that claimed capitalism and technology should be expedited so that humankind could emancipate itself from planet Earth, comparing it to the theory of perpetual motion. After all, where would we get the necessary material substrate for this change of address to the stars?

I read into dawn. All those stacks of paper would be of

little use to the biography, a paragraph at most, or a page at the end of the book about the author's final days. But reading it rattled me so much that I had my first bout of serious insomnia in weeks. As day broke, my eyes were still open, and I walked back and forth from the bed to the sofa, trying to understand why Duke, Duke of all people, had let himself be duped by that deluge of apocalyptic fancies. Maybe what he'd wanted was precisely to condemn such catastrophism as no more than the latest nihilist trend. We'd never know. In any case, the sun was rising and the cars had once again started clogging up the street beneath my window when I finally made the connection between everything I had just read and Aurora's recent mood. Our conversation on the day of the funeral, and later on the phone, had made me fear for her state of mind. More than Duke's research, it was the memory of her surrender to that feeling of doom that had affected me to the point of scaring away sleep. I smiled at the thought that Andrei's unfinished novel could have been about her, or better yet, about people like her, neither old nor young enough to escape the pitfalls of pessimism at that point in human history. I walked like a zombie through the streets of the Petrópolis neighborhood, startling grandmas walking their dogs and forcing joggers in sportswear to dodge me on their way to the park or gym. I walked to a bakery called Lancheria do Parque, where I ordered a glass of watermelon juice and some salami toast. The elderly men who took their breakfast there were at their usual tables, with their cups of coffee and shriveled pastels, watching the growing bustle around them. They would stay there until noon, with nothing better to do. The same old men. The same old thing. For the past fifteen, twenty years.

As soon as I was done eating, my exhaustion hit me in full. If I went to sleep at that time in the morning, I'd just trigger another night of insomnia, followed by a whole string of them. I'd been rid of that shit for weeks. I went home again and found non-intellectual things to occupy myself with. I found two relevant papers on the kitchen table. A notice for the delivery of a package to the post office and a letter from the bank recommending I renegotiate the debt on my last credit card. That was exactly what I needed, documents containing missions. I took a cold shower, grabbed the two notes, and took the bus to the center of town. First, the post office. Chaos reigned at the distribution center because of a workers' strike that had ended just a few days earlier. A dozen customers demanded information on their delayed packages. The heat and armpit stink brought to mind the expression "the anteroom of hell," which I had read in a Thomas Bernhard book. A man began crying at a clerk who was screaming that he didn't know where his package was. A young guy with a patchy moustache whined that the iPad he had ordered two months ago was being held at the post office. He couldn't be any more than eighteen years old, and yet there he was, already a full-fledged hipster. Back in my day, a pubescent moustache and red-framed glasses were the height of uncool. A surefire way to get beat up and find yourself the object of pity, regardless of age or gender. But this kid had probably been dabbling in polyamory since he was fourteen. I asked him if he'd heard of Atari. The pipsqueak said he had played it at an arcade bar he sometimes went to. And Odyssey? He hadn't heard of it. It predates Atari, motherfucker, I thought. The mail clerk, an obese black man in need of a shave, called my number. He was even sweatier and more desperate than the customers clamoring for their packages. I felt sorry for him. He handed me a small, beat-up package that might as well have had the words "debut book" scrawled across it. I ripped off the brown paper wrapping. It was exactly that. *Frisson.* Poetry. People sent me this kind of book because of reviews I published here and there, and also because of *Orangutan*. It amazed me that publishers still had my address on their mailing lists because of an e-zine from fifteen years ago. I placed the book in my backpack and walked a few blocks until I reached Banco do Brasil on Rua Siqueira Campos. Micaela, the manager, had gold-lacquered nails and a gold watch. There were graphite highlights in her dyed hair, which was so perfectly straightened it looked like synthetic fabric. Her perfume was vanilla and yerba maté and had been applied with a generosity diametrically opposed to that of the banking system. Due to criminal interest rates, my debt of approximately two thousand reals had quadrupled to eight thousand, but I left there owing only the original two thousand, in twelve installments. With the advance I was getting for the biography, I'd be financially stable, at least for a few months.

Energized by all the pending issues I'd managed to square away, I not only forgot my exhaustion but was gripped by an unusual disposition. It was just past noon. Instead of getting lunch, I rode the bus home, shoved my goggles, swimming briefs, towel, and other accoutrements into my backpack, and took the T9 bus to the athletic center at the Pontifical Catholic University of Rio Grande do Sul. I arrived there at around one fifteen, when the pool was usually empty. I paid thirty reals for the day pass and swam in the Olympic lane for forty minutes, alternating between front crawl and backstroke, stopping to rest every two to three hundred meters. It had been months since I'd last gone swimming, due to apathy and for reasons of cost containment. I still lifted weights and sometimes I ran and used the exercise bars at Parque da Redenção, but my swimming stamina had atrophied considerably, and my arms and shoulders were slack and ached a little. I left gobs of smoker's phlegm throughout the pool, coughing hard underwater, entertained by the explosions of bubbles. On my way out, I lay on a foam mat on the pool's edge and did some sit-ups. I stayed there for a while, panting, inhaling the scent of chlorine and foot odor fouling up the space and savoring the endorphins as if I had just taken ecstasy.

In the locker room, a group of four douchebags cracked jokes about the few women who swam during their time slot. No one was spared, not the hot teacher who had been fired, the young piece swimming laps in the free lane, or the custodian who cleaned their floor. The group was composed of two decrepit fatsos, a gangly beanpole, and a guy who looked like a jock and had patches of vitiligo around his ribs and hands. One of the fatsos started howling about how he was going to file a formal complaint with the priests who owned the university, protesting the excess of men in the athletic center's pool. They all laughed their asses off. As much as I supported the objectification of people for sexual ends, I was continually astounded by the banality and idiocy of men fraternizing in locker rooms. What offended me was not turning others—men or women—into objects of desire but doing so with poor wit and a lack of imagination. I myself, it has to be said, was eyeing the stud with vitiligo as if he were a hunk of meat. Out of the corner of my eye, of course. If I could have opened my mouth without the risk of being lynched, I would have said something far more creative than the crap I was hearing. But they weren't paying me any attention. Desiring men in men's locker rooms demanded a talent for invisibility I'd been perfecting for years. You had to be careful not to let yourself be fooled by the open camaraderie and excess of physical affection that came naturally to certain straight men, behavior that grossly resembled an overture. Men in men's locker rooms brazenly massaged each other's egos, certain that in that space, no matter what they did, they'd never be taken for fags. When the guy's swimming briefs came off, I glimpsed patches of vitiligo on his dick and couldn't help getting the onset of an erection. I'd never seen anything like it. My reaction was visceral. Though my cock didn't rise, it swelled. I hid it with a towel, pulled my shorts from my backpack, and quickly got dressed, without properly drying off. The physical evidence out of sight, I continued to fantasize while I finished getting dressed. I'd start by turning to face them, cock stiff, and be met with instant disgust and indignation. The fat guys and the beanpole wouldn't have the guts to confront me, but the one with vitiligo would come at me swinging, which was exactly what I wanted. I'd slap him around a bit and then immobilize him. After which I would eat his ass out on the filthy floor, wet and carpeted in pubes. I'd grind his face into the ground. At some point, he would give in and start enjoying it. The others would have already fled. Sounds of outrage would travel down the building's hallways. The athletic center's security guards would burst into the locker room, truncheons in hand and walkie-talkies screeching, only to catch me choking on his white-spotted cock. At which point the brawl would really kick off.

This connection between sex and violence was no mystery to me. It had been born, I thought, in those years when I'd refused to accept that the aesthetic admiration I felt toward men was actually a desire for them. I'd been a good fighter since I was a kid. In my early high school years, I used to punch my schoolmates in the arm just so I could see them cry or, better yet, so that they would fight back. Later, I got into scraps with anybody who responded to a provocation. More than drawing blood, what gave me pleasure was to immobilize the other kids, to drag them to the ground in an armlock or another similar maneuver, until someone pulled me off them or until our strength drained from our bodies, the confrontation ending out of pure physical necessity. Now, all these years later, I was able to put myself in my schoolmates' shoes and see just how peculiar those brawls would have seemed to them, with their undertows of ulterior motives that no one could name. I only recognized my urges for what they really were after that night with Andrei. The irony of our encounter, the ironic rejection I'd been subjected to, added the final component into my relationship with men. Rage. I wasn't a sadist, exactly, but I got a kick out of imposing power, out of unilaterally and steadily doling out small doses of physical pain. This is why I was attracted to virile men. For a long time, I didn't quite know what to do with those desires.

In the years that followed that night in Duke's apartment, after the party at Bar Ocidente, I developed the unhealthy habit of fixing my eyes until the very last moment on men who interested me, regardless of whether they were gay or not. I even preferred the obviously straight ones, those men who felt hatred and repulsion and would undoubtedly punch back. Before I'd become acquainted with the gay nightlife of Porto Alegre, I used to try my hand at this in the bars of Avenida Goethe and Rua da República, at parks in the light of day, and at the cafés where I had my morning coffee and a ham-and-cheese sandwich. Of course, the response was nearly always hostile, and so I would find myself shifting, in the blink of an eye, from lechery to violence. I would astutely craft the conditions that justified violence. I won every fight. I took pleasure in scraping my fists on the teeth of the same men I'd just been hitting on. The pleasure of sex was so rare I taught myself to mistake it for the pleasure of aggression. Virility, I was beginning to understand, was a resource that could be channeled into tenderness and violence with equal effectiveness and with a payoff similarly intense in terms of the end-sensations. One year, when I was with my parents at a summer rental in Imbé, I was attacked by two men at once in front of a strip of bars crammed with seasonal visitors. One of them hit me in the face with a belt, its buckle opening a cut near my eye. A larger group started gathering around me to kick my faggot ass. I managed to run home. This was the first time I became concerned about the territory I was treading and considered finding a therapist or some sort of help. I was just shy of thirty, a sought-after freelance journalist. I'd end up getting myself killed because of the kinds of neuroses that seemed better-suited to a troubled teenager.

Sometime later, one of my seductive looks was taken differently by André, whom I met at a college friend's wedding. I felt as if I could have looked at him for the rest of my life. For weeks, I spent more nights at his apartment than I did at my own. He was a DJ and had the habit of coming home drunk, either at sunrise or when the sun was already bright in the sky. Sometimes, in bed, he'd enter a strange state of alcohol-induced somnambulism in which he had to fuck at any cost. Usually rested and lucid, I'd feel like I was having sex with a malfunctioning droid, if not a corpse. André would mumble semi-coherent nonsense in a monotonous tone, lewd phrases like those of an erotic film, but with neither any emotion nor modulation to his voice, as if he were narrating someone else's actions. His body and mind seemed dissociated. I would remember André most on my nights of insomnia, when my body and mind also felt disconnected, trapped in experiences that were not only separate but incompatible. André was my first requited love. What I had wanted from Duke two years earlier. Though our relationship only lasted about three months, it mollified me. After him, I stopped getting into fights on the street whenever I was lusting after a man. Even so, in my inner world, those two things, desire and physical violence, remained bound together. And I liked to nurture that bond. I found it beautiful. I liked seeing myself from the outside and knowing that this was the kind of person I was. It made me proud. I was, I supposed, what people commonly referred to as a self-possessed man.

I got home, ordered a bacon cheeseburger for delivery, poured a strong coffee into my IBOPE promo mug and sat at my computer. I spent an hour organizing the material I had already collected for the biography into folders. Then, I transcribed relevant passages from my conversations with Francine and Antero. My interview with Antero had revealed little I hadn't already known about Duke. Antero was too egocentric to remember in detail anything that didn't directly involve him. His most interesting anecdote was about the time he and Duke had tried to write an interactive story together for online publication. The end result had been shit, in his opinion, and the piece was never posted. Even so, the experience had allowed him to witness Duke's creative process from up close. Duke didn't like doing drafts or writing up plans. He would only start typing his piece once it had already been conceived in detail in his imagination. The first draft was definitive. This had been one of their issues, because Antero had wanted to map out the plot and all its ramifications, to write up character charts, create lists of significant concepts, gather JPEGs for visual references. All the while, Duke remained quiet, mentally machinating. After that story and another couple of mostly useless anecdotes, Antero started doing what he knew best. Talking about himself. And that day he had something to talk about. As we sat a table in the Lagom Brewery on Rua Bento Figueiredo, I noted the absence of his characteristic effusion.

"Giane kicked me out of the house," he blurted out as soon as the waiter brought us our pints of craft blonde ale.

"Bah," I limited myself to saying. Just then, I recalled the night of the funeral and couldn't help asking. "Aurora?"

He was taken aback by the mention of her name and frowned like an attorney who has caught an inconsistency in a deposition.

"Sorry, man, but I've been around a long time," I added. "I was minding my own business, but it was clear where that night was heading."

"Yeah, there was that, too," he said, relaxing again. "But that wasn't what Giane found. A girl in São Paulo who I went out with a couple of times sent her a Facebook message. With photos."

"That's rough."

"And then she posted something public, and other women did, too. Anyway. The whole situation's ugly, I can't even bring myself to think about it."

In the course of the following three rounds of beer, while Antero tried his best to say something useful about Duke, I was trying to decide, in the back of my mind, whether he deserved my empathy. Antero was rich and did as he damn well pleased. One word from him and businessmen scrapped campaigns and products into which they'd already sunk millions. He was the only one of us who'd been in a long-term relationship, the only one with a kid. How then could he seem so fragile, so ridiculous to me? He didn't seem to be coping well with the fact that he had an adult body. That the people around him were adults. He'd taken on the pear-shaped build common to so many successful admen. I was sure that when Antero looked in the mirror, what he saw was 1999 Antero, a young man for whom life's demands and the constraints of the material world weren't worthy of consideration. Without his wife and son, Antero seemed to have suffered a sudden and rude awakening. I decided that yes, he did deserve my empathy. That same tenderness I felt so easily for Aurora, the desire that she be happy in the future, manifested itself before this Antero who bit his nails and checked his phone every twenty seconds.

"If you talk to Aurora, tell her to call or email me," Antero said as we shook hands outside the bar. "She won't talk to me anymore, and I don't know why."

"Man, I don't know if it's my place to say this, but . . . go apologize to your wife. Forget Aurora."

"You don't know what it's like."

"Don't know what what's like?"

He shrugged his shoulders and said nothing. I thought he'd turn around and leave, but he just stood there, like a kid abandoned by his parents. And then I had a thought.

"Where are you staying?"

"I slept at a buddy's place last night, but some guys are Airbnbing it today. I'm going to find a hotel."

"If you don't mind a sofa bed, you can crash at mine."

That night, we drained half a bottle of Jim Beam and

every beer in the fridge. He scrounged a half-dozen cigarettes off me and killed the end of a spliff he had in his wallet. We confessed things about our emotional lives, concluded that love was no easy matter and shouldn't be treated like it was, talked trash like a couple of kids, and vented our frustrations and prejudices. We watched the infamous film he made in the nineties. He'd lost the file years ago. After playing it five times in a row, he sank into a deep silence that lasted more than a minute.

"Andrei shot that," he finally mumbled, his tongue stumbling.

"I know."

"Man, we were such retards."

I laughed.

"That's one way of looking at it, for sure."

I don't know exactly when we went to sleep, but it was well after midnight. Around seven in the morning, Antero knocked on the door to my room. It was overcast, and still looked like night.

"Giane texted," he said without looking at me, leaning against the doorframe, his thumbs typing with frenetic vigor. "She wants to talk. Can you open the door to let me out?"

I cursed under my breath as I got out of bed, wearing only my briefs, and went to open the door. He typed a bit more, lifted his eyes from the screen for an instant, and smiled at me sadly.

"Make me look good in Duke's bio, hey?"

He ran out, without saying goodbye. He didn't seem hungover. How was that even possible? He'd be a teenager till the end of his days, I thought. I stood listening to the sounds of his steps on the staircase, then the door slammed shut. For some reason, I knew we would never see each other again.

As soon as I finished typing up my notes from my conversation with Antero, I went out for a pack of cigarettes. I saw a stray dog peeing on another stray dog taking a dump. Back in my office, I smoked and stretched my neck, shoulders, and forearms, the parts of my body that were most affected by tendinitis if I wasn't careful. Swimming had left me with an insatiable hunger. I opened a bag of Doritos and a liter-bottle of expired Patricia beer that I'd bought on sale at the Public Market. Half an hour later, I was ready to write again. I looked for the notes I'd taken two days earlier during my conversation with Sara, Duke's mother. Her son's death was still fresh, and she was unsettled by the idea of a biography. I said it was a big undertaking. It was important I get started soon so that I could produce something worthy of Duke. She softened when I started recalling stories from our *Orangutan* days, the barbecues, the first couple of newspaper articles about our electronic fanzine. She showed me the newspaper clippings she had kept in a folder. There we were, Duke, Antero, Aurora, and me, and a few other contributors, posing like rock stars at the photographer's request. Unlike all of them, who were perfectly suited to that scene—young, smooth, rosy, with nothing to lose—I looked completely out of place in the far corner of that photograph, the oldest geezer in the group, a grown-up man with a face pockmarked by acne. Antero used to call me Kátia Flávia, because he thought I looked like Fausto Fawcett. I'd put up with it, even though I couldn't see the resemblance at the time. As I looked at the photo, I thought Antero had been right, in a way. I did look a bit like a Fausto Fawcett without glasses.

I decided to focus on Duke's family history, sidestepping his life altogether. We could pick that up some other time, in a few months. Sara showed me an old photograph taken in Buenos Aires of Andrei's great-grandparents, which was affixed to a piece of card with an embossed pattern stained by time. His great-grandmother Elena, in a dress with white gloves, oval-framed eyeglasses, and a tiara perched on her wavy hair, stood in front of a wooden folding screen. His great-grandfather Jacobo Dukelsky wore a black buttoned-up jacket with a white tie and a Nikolai II style moustache. They had emigrated from different parts of Russia and had met onboard a ship bound for Buenos Aires. A baron by the name of Hirsch lived in the Argentine capital and used his fortune to help Russian Jews fleeing military service or pogroms. Elena and Jacobo were married and followed the baron when he decided to establish a Jewish community in the middle of an inhospitable *pampas* in Brazil. That community gave rise to a city called Quatro Irmãos, or Four Brothers. Elena, according to Sara, always wore a pearl necklace and high-heeled shoes, even in the middle of that primitive land, and after a few years began managing the grocery store her family opened in town. Jacobo always wore a suit and tie to work construction on the local railway. When the government sent him a sack of seeds to sow, he dug an enormous hole and buried the entire sack. My notes on Duke's great-grandparents filled several pages of my small notebook. There was no information on the rest of the family. Sara had tired of talking, and so we agreed to schedule another meeting. In between older stories of Jewish immigrants in southern Brazil and the reality of Duke's death, the posthumous mythos surrounding him, and his persistence in the media, online, in universities, in bookstores and in libraries, loomed a gigantic void that would need to be filled. The book had potential. And I would be a sort of guardian to Duke's history. The person responsible for providing a solid, faithful account of his life, the gold standard for everything that would later be written about him.

I wrote for an hour and a half, describing how Elena and Jacobo might have met aboard the ship carrying them from Russia. I spent another half hour Googling Russia in the 1920s. I was so wired I didn't notice night fall. I hadn't slept in nearly two days, and yet I was buzzing. I saved the file and wrapped things up for the day. Before turning off my computer, I logged on to Facebook. Just a quick look. From their solitary observation posts in the sea of things polemical and viral, the children of the millennium shot signals into the sky and threw messages in bottles out to sea. The self-esteem of all depended on people's possible responses. Manfredo, for example, had posted YouTube videos of songs by Bonnie "Prince" Billy and Apanhador Só, with needy comments indirectly for my benefit. I clicked "like" on all of them. Meanwhile, there were twenty-six unread messages in my Messenger inbox. It took me over an hour to respond to each of them. One was from Francine: "I was left feeling like I'd said both too much and too little. Above all, I'm thinking of Andrei and of how to respect his wishes. I'd like it if you saw me as a friend and ally, not an obstacle. Xx." I sent back a friendly response and opened her photo album. She told me she had deleted all of the photos of her and Andrei together. In fact, there were only about a dozen images, and she was alone in nearly all of them. There was a photo of her as a teenager beside an English Setter, another where she was smoking a hookah with her sister in Amsterdam. Her sister wore a nose ring and had a soft face that, in contrast, accentuated Francine's more masculine features.

I kept wondering whether Francine's virtual cleanup of Andrei's data had really been that thorough. She didn't strike me as particularly knowledgeable about the internet. It's not like she was a web nerd. Unlike Duke, who had published his first pieces on websites he built himself, some of them small works of art in HTML and GIF form, investigating the possible layouts and typographies offered by the programming languages of the time. With a nagging suspicion on my mind, I opened the homepage for the website that hosted the blog Francine was unable to access. I typed in his Gmail username, dukdukelsky. He probably used the same username for other sites. I watched the cursor blinking in the blank password box. I remembered Francine mentioning that Duke had created his passwords out of acronyms formed from the opening lines of novels and short stories. Only then did I realize how strange it was that she had shared this information with me. I felt as if she and Duke were inviting me to help solve a puzzle.

I grabbed my cellphone and scrolled through the photos I'd taken of Duke's books. Most of the spines were legible when I zoomed in. I scoured the photos for books he had mentioned throughout his life, either in conversation or in interviews, books that had affected or marked him in some way. I ruled out any new releases or editions that I knew to be too recent, since the blog's password would have been created several years ago. The first posts dated to 2006. I tried to pinpoint books that might have been on Duke's mind at the time. But that wasn't enough. The books in question had to be on my own shelves, too, so I could check their opening sentences. This drastically narrowed the set of results, but not enough to deter me. The first book to pass scrutiny was *À mão esquerda*, by Fausto Wolff. Duke and I had loved that deranged, mythomaniacal book and used to talk about it all the time. I pulled my copy off the shelf. The first sentence read, "My brother Pérsio has been a journalist since he was a boy." I jotted down the acronym. I continued studying the spines in the photographs. *Sun and Steel*, by Yukio Mishima, translated into Portuguese by Paulo Leminski. I was the one who'd recommended it to Duke. Together, we had tracked down his copy at Beco dos Livros, a secondhand bookstore on Rua General Câmara. The book had bowled me over, and we'd often found ourselves talking about it. The opening sentence was long. "Of late, I have come to sense within myself an accumulation of all kinds of things that cannot find adequate expression via an objective artistic form such as the novel." If this were the matrix for his password, he would probably have used only the first eight to ten letters. The next book to meet the criteria was *La pesquisa*, by Juan José Saer. It had been published in Portuguese in 1999, and I remembered reading it during the golden days of our *Orangutan* parties. It had been one of Duke's recommendations. "Instead, there, in December, night falls fast," read the first sentence. Seven letters. As I found the books, I typed up the acronyms of the opening lines in a Notepad document. I came up with fourteen passwords based on eight books.

I was well aware that my chances of getting it right were microscopic, so it didn't frustrate me when none of the passwords worked on the blog. Even if I put every book in Duke's library through this process, it was highly unlikely I'd come up with his actual password. Even so, the game I was playing only intensified the feeling I had of following clues left behind by the deceased author. I felt my pulse beating at my temple. I was in a frenzy. My glands shot natural crack into my bloodstream. An absolutely unwarranted, stubborn erection bulged at the seams of my briefs. What a day for my penis. I hadn't had erections at that rate since riding the bus as a teenager. I tried to think of other websites on which he might have opened an account, ones that might not have found their way into the will Francine had read after his death. Profiles Duke himself might have forgotten about. I tried unsuccessfully to log on to StumbleUpon and Myspace, two sites that people used a lot in the early 2000s but had since been forgotten. I also tried out the set of passwords on Formspring, a question-and-answer site that was once a huge success but whose popularity had fallen with the rise of the comparable ASKfm. One of the last interviews Duke gave before he stopped talking to the press was a three-day marathon on Formspring. He'd answered any and every question he received, so long as it avoided personal matters involving people close to him. It was a tour de force. In one fell swoop, he'd exploded notions of privacy, of the place of the author, and of the possibilities of the interview, and then forever withdrawn from the media and the public eye. This had taken place in either 2008 or 2009, I couldn't quite remember, but the end result of that experiment remained available online for a few years, until he himself took it down, or so it was presumed. A number of people probably had copies. I, at least, had kept mine on my hard drive. The questions and answers were arranged in a text file of nearly one megabyte, ranging from topics such as the inspiration for his characters, his political convictions and philosophical views, to the frequency with which he clipped his nails and his most embarrassing experiences. It was endless. Duke's promise in Formspring's banner was to be unshakably honest, but how was anyone to know? Those who knew him well suspected that, counter to what he'd promised, he'd been more interested in constructing a narrative of fictional contours than he was in sticking to the truth. In any case, Formspring also rejected every one of my username-and-password combos. I also tried them on pornographic websites and online stores, as well as crowdfunding and file-sharing sites.

I was about to call it quits when I decided to try his username and password on SprintRun, a running app. According to Francine, Duke used to work out nearly every day. He'd been assaulted on one of his nightly jogs through the city. The robber had taken his iPhone. He probably had a running app, and SprintRun was the most popular one. Typing on autopilot, my vision already blurred, I entered the passwords one by one, and then pressed Enter. At some point, the screen didn't refresh with an "incorrect username or password" but instead loaded another page full of charts, menus, and JPEGs of happy people running. Skeptical, I scrolled from top to bottom. I was in Duke's account. His name and photo were displayed in his profile box in the top left corner of the screen. Jewish nose and prematurely bald head, penetrating eyes and thick lips, a five-o'clock shadow. A workout timeline occupied the center of the screen, with meteorological and geographical icons illustrating whether it had rained or shined on the day of his run, if the path he had taken was on asphalt, track, or dirt, displaying such information as the duration of his jog, the distance traveled, and his average speed. Each item was also accompanied by a miniature map on which his cellphone's GPS had traced the outline of his route. The user profile was on the right-hand side of the screen. Andrei Dukelsky, Porto Alegre (RS), gender male, single, intermediate level, date of birth January 12, 1978. An animated banner capped the same column. "RUNNING IS LIFE! Become a GOLD member—Achieve your goals—25% OFF." It was too late for him, I thought. In the half-darkness of SprintRun's servers was an algorithm-controlled database that remained indifferent to life or death.

On the bar at the top of the screen was a menu listing options such as Routes, Statistics, Friends, and Activities. I clicked on Statistics. In January 2014, from the first of the month until the day he died, Duke had jogged 112 kilometers in 10 hours and 17 minutes and burned 9,461 calories. Since he had first started using the app, he had jogged more than 3,500 kilometers and burned nearly 300,000 calories. His cumulative elevation gain was 29 kilometers, with a markedly similar figure in elevation loss. It was as if he'd gone up and down Mount Everest more than three times. Then, I clicked on Routes. There were half a dozen recorded routes in Porto Alegre. Four left Duke's apartment on Avenida José Bonifácio and went along various avenues and through nearby parks. One of his routes went down Avenida Beira Rio, from Usina do Gasômetro to the Iberê Camargo Museum. Another was an extension of the former, starting at his house and stretching all the way to Avenida Beira Rio. There were various treks through cities across Brazil and the world. He'd probably never missed a chance to go for a run whenever he attended literary events out-of-state or abroad. Those red outlines drew geometric forms and irregular scrawls through capitals such as Stockholm, Berlin, Madrid, Paris, Washington, D.C., Bogotá. There was a route in Luanda. New Delhi. Two in São Paulo. One in Rio de Janeiro, around Rodrigo de Freitas Lagoon, departing from an address in Humaitá and circling back to it.

I returned to the first page. The first map on his timeline outlined Duke's itinerary on the night he died. The route left his apartment, opposite Parque da Redenção, and cut through the middle of the park, passing by the fountain and the water mirror, running up Rua Tomaz Flores and veering left onto Vasco da Gama, which it followed all the way to Colégio Rosário. Then, it looped around Praça Dom Sebastião and traveled up the entirety of Avenida Independência, took Rua 24 de Outubro to Parque Moinhos de Vento, which it cut straight through, and continued along Avenida Goethe and Rua Silva Só until it reached Avenida Protásio Alves. And then something strange and unsettling occurred. Instead of going right on Protásio and turning back to his point of departure on Avenida José Bonifácio, Duke went left, jogging along the sidewalk for a few blocks until he arrived at Rua Vicente da Fontoura, where he went left, crossed Rua Passo da Pátria and came to a stop right in front of my building. Then, he did a one-eighty, ran back along Protásio, and took the shortest route home.

I stared at the map for a while, dumbfounded. I hadn't stepped away from my computer in five hours. I went to the living room for a glass of whisky and then back. It was eleven thirty at night. As rattled, worn-out, and manic as I might have been feeling, there was no other way to read that map. On the day a robber had shot him dead, Duke took a detour that led him to my apartment building. An obvious detour. The outline itself illustrated as much. A strange, L-shaped form jutted out from a closed circuit, leaving behind wide footpaths and parks and probing the narrow, run-down sidewalks of Avenida Protásio Alves, only to reach the front steps of my building and turn back.

But that wasn't all. The route captured by the GPS on the night of the assault didn't stop near Hospital de Clínicas, on the corner of Avenida Protásio Alves and Rua Ramiro Barcelos, where Duke was murdered. Instead, the line on the map crossed Protásio and went three blocks up Ramiro Barcelos, until it reached the viaduct over Rua Vasco da Gama. It was possible that the app or the phone's GPS had glitched. Or maybe it was showing the robber's escape route. The murderer could have deactivated the GPS. Or damaged the cellphone. The entire trek had amounted to just over nine kilometers. It had lasted an hour and nineteen minutes, which probably reflected how long the app had been on for. The app had logged an average of 151 heartbeats per minute. Was it possible that the heart monitor strapped to Duke's chest had tracked the drop in his heartbeats until it came to a complete stop?

As I scrolled down his timeline, my eyes scanned all the routes Duke had jogged in the previous months. The one he'd taken the day he died was also the most common. In certain cases, the detour that led him to my building was clearly visible. It wasn't often, but it was there. I continued scrolling. Four. Five. Six. Ten times. At some point, I stopped checking. Those mysterious visits, if it made sense to call them that, generally occurred during his night runs, between eight and nine p.m., but also sometimes in the mornings or afternoons. It was difficult to determine whether I'd been at home each of these times. After all, my routine wasn't the least bit regular. Duke had never rung the intercom while I was in, that much I knew for sure. My room and office windows faced the street. But I didn't have a clear view of the sidewalk from the second floor. What's more, because I preferred dark spaces, I often opened the shutters no more than a crack to let some of the cigarette smoke slip out. Had I seen him on one of the times I had stood outside the window watching the bustle below me? Had I ever returned to my computer with the hazy sensation that I had spied Duke in sneakers and running shorts? I pictured him standing down there, panting and dripping with sweat in the humid Porto Alegre air, shirtless, baring his hairy back, looking up at my window for a few minutes and then leaving again. For years we had communicated exclusively by email. We'd seen each other once at a party in 2012. A year before his death, we had met for coffee after a chance run-in at the Porto Alegre Book Fair. I'd been interviewing a Cuban author who was passing through town. He had come to pan for sales, like all of us Orangutans had in the past. We cheerfully reminisced, over coffee, on the titles we used to find on sale at the Book Fair back in the nineties. Since the books came in large batches of remainders, we'd often all end up buying the same ones. Picturesque gems such as *Phutatorius*, by Jaime Rodrigues, and *Novel with Cocaine*, by M. Ageyev. That was where I last saw Duke in person. I decided, for lack of any better theories, that the detours Duke had taken to my building during his jogs had sprung from a deep personal need. That they were part of his *secret life*, in other words, part of the habits we cultivated alone that, though they may appear absurd from any practical standpoint, were nonetheless absolutely essential to us. Every Monday, I got lunch at the same lousy restaurant because I found its atmosphere and clientele inexplicably comforting and thought it fostered self-reflection. I'd end many nights out drinking at a lackluster bar on Rua General Lima e Silva, where, years earlier, I'd had a pleasant discussion with a straight man about the fallacious top/bottom dichotomy of homoerotic contexts. Even though there was nothing particularly special about that bar, a dive where nothing ever happened, it felt good to return there, think back on that amicable conversation, and inhabit the realm of pleasant expectations that I knew, in advance, would never be requited. These sorts of things were a part of my secret life. According to SprintRun's logs, Duke's included looking up at my window from time to time. Regardless of whether my interpretation was correct, the idea of it pressed on my heart with such force that my eyes welled with tears.

I went out a little after midnight. I walked along Avenida Protásio Alves until I reached the intersection where Duke had been killed, and then turned right on Ramiro Barcelos. I walked three blocks to the viaduct that ran over Rua Vasco da Gama, passing by a new craft beer bar with a food truck parked out front. Up on the viaduct, I spent a few minutes staring down at the traffic below. Taxi after taxi sped toward the bars in Bom Fim and Cidade Baixa. A group of girls whose hair was either short or shaved at the sides pedaled fixies with carefree agility down Ramiro Barcelos and up the pedestrian pass beside the viaduct. An elderly man walked down the sidewalk with a fat, quaking dog. The absence of parked cars pointed at the likelihood that they would be broken into or stolen at gunpoint in that part of town. In the recently renovated square beside the viaduct, a group of four youths in baseball caps smoked weed and listened to baile funk on their cellphones. There was noise, but also long moments of silence. It had been years since that nighttime bustle had taken on a clandestine air. Being out on the streets was daring, maybe even political. In that moment, I joined the ranks of the incautious who stubbornly affirmed the existence of a public nightlife outside of outings to late-night movie screenings at shopping mall cinemas. Without wasting another moment, I walked along the access ramps and pedestrian passes that connected the footpath on Rua Vasco da Gama to the Ramiro viaduct. The shrubbery was varied and hadn't been tended to in a while. Unhurriedly, lit cigarette in mouth, I rifled through the turf and the grass bordering the sidewalk and pried open bush branches. I found a gray woolen glove. Then, a few chicken bones, a Styrofoam box with age-old leftovers, a pair of headphones, a small dead bird, a tied-up bag of dog shit. I had to find all that junk before I could be persuaded Duke's stolen cellphone wasn't there. The path of his last run had come to an end in that place either because his phone had died or because the robber had switched it off. After so many clues and revelations, it was hard to accept I had hit a wall. The trail had ended in an abyss. I walked at a clip toward Bom Fim, headed for nothing in particular.

At moments, I felt Duke's nonexistent phone pulsing in my left pants pocket. I even went so far as to reach into it and check that it was still empty. It was the same phantom vibration I sometimes felt on my right thigh, where I usually kept my own cell. That illusion, I thought, was the culmination of what had started with my research into his passwords, into the running app, my rummaging in the bushes. Something unmentionable yet nonetheless related to Duke's persistence in that software and on those streets, beyond his obvious persistence in the memories and hearts of those who'd known him personally. The Vasco da Gama viaduct seemed to remember him like I did. The miniature maps of his jogging routes on SprintRun seemed to lament his passing much like his devoted readers. Saer's book, which had provided the code for one of his passwords, seemed proud of that connection. Those objects and things, those places and patterns of digital information, seemed to have been changed by his death like I had. They had, in other words, been affected.

I was spiraling to the end of that train of thought when my phone actually vibrated in my right pocket. I glanced around me. I was heading down Avenida Independência toward the city center, passing Bambu's. From the corner where I stood, gazing out at Rua Barros Cassal, my eyes fell on the now-defunct Garagem Hermética, once the site of many an *Orangutan* party, and now a venue for mainstream gigs ranging from college *sertanejo* groups to Pink Floyd cover bands. I couldn't remember what route I had followed to arrive there. I'd been walking on autopilot for at least fifteen minutes. I opened the WhatsApp message I'd just received. It was from Aurora. "Hey Êmi. Remember that time we talked about your family's ranch, where we spent New Year's Eve in '99? Could I go there for a few days? It's been on my mind. Xx"

I sat on the curb by a hot dog truck serving a young couple in party attire, a guy in a gas station uniform, and a cross-dressing garbage collector. The scent of boiled sausage was as nauseating as it was nostalgic. My initial urge was to tell Aurora about Duke's runs. No. Mentioning his visits to that sidewalk was a terrible idea, I decided. I could foresee the skepticism in her response and was scared it might destroy me. I got up and ordered a hot dog, no cheese. I texted Aurora while I waited. "We can make it work. Are you coming down to Porto Alegre on vacation? Let's hammer out the details when I'm in São Paulo." The app informed me that my message had been sent. Then it informed me that it had been received. Seconds later, it informed me that Aurora was typing. Another ten seconds later, the little response bubble appeared. "If you can't make it, I could go on my own. I still have that .txt file with directions on how to get there by car. If that's alright, of course." I remembered sending the entire gang a .txt file with detailed instructions on how to get there from the Guaíba drawbridge, with kilometer markers and visual references for changes in the dirt road. Her allusion to the file filled me with the same sense of time-travel as Antero's video. A fifteen-year-old digital file filled me with the same sense of awe as the four-billion-year-old Martian meteorite that had been discovered in Antarctica and contained microscopic fossils of alien bacteria almost as old as the solar system itself. Much like the meteorite, the file hinted at a past impossible to imagine. Fifteen years. Before cellphones with inbuilt cameras. Even before digital cameras. If there was any evidence on film of our camping trip to the ranch, I wasn't aware of it. The text file Aurora had kept, however, was testament to the fact that, yes, we had spent the turn of the millennium in the wild, at a safe distance from modernity, from fireworks, and from civilization's possible collapse. "It's no trouble at all. But let's go together. I don't like the idea of you being there on your own," I typed back.

Aurora was slow to respond. My hot dog arrived first. It was terrible, as expected. Moist, soft bread. Pale, bland sausages. Overly sweet, watery ketchup. Corn and peas that looked like they'd been preserved in enema fluid. Rubbery shoestring potatoes that stuck to your teeth. Smegma mayo.

The salsa had frozen. And, even though it wasn't on my bun, the grated Parmesan let off a sharp odor from its plastic container in the van. The hot dog's entrails dribbled out on first bite. I devoured every last bit. I was starting on my third sleepless night. Oddly enough, I no longer felt manic, but instead alert and awake. Maybe a bit delirious. It was hard to tell for sure. I wiped my hands on the wax paper, which only managed to spread the mayonnaise and grease around some more.

I completed the task with my shirt and again took out my cellphone. Aurora had continued to text me while I ate my hot dog. "The world's ending now, Êmi. It might have already ended in São Paulo, in Porto Alegre. It'll take longer to reach the ranch." Then: "I don't want to scare you, it's just a manner of speaking. I need to get away for a while. I'd like to spend a few weeks there, if that's alright with you and your parents." The messages became increasingly troubling. "It might even be better for me to spend a few days there on my own. Don't worry, I'm not thinking of doing anything stupid." Then: "I'm going to take an archery class. A guy I hooked up with recently has been doing it for months and he's going to take me." And ended with: "Alright, I'll let you sleep." I lit a cigarette to cleanse my palate. Part of me wanted to call Aurora and gently chide her. But if I called her, I'd just end up talking about the password and those secret visitations. I needed to tell someone, just not Aurora. Who could

I tell? Where was that path taking me, what was on the other side of that wall? I typed a string of words and then deleted them until finally settling on "Don't turn away from the light, Aurora. We'll discuss the ranch when I'm in São Paulo. It'll all work out. I need to go now. Take care, xx" She ended our chat with "O.k. xx"

A half hour later, I was ringing Duke's intercom. Without asking what I wanted, Francine unlocked the door to the building, which had neither a doorman nor an elevator. As I climbed the flights of stairs, I considered turning back. Rather than ring the bell, I tapped gently on the door. She greeted me, a light jacket over her nightie. The left side of her face was creased, either by a blanket or a pillow. Her countenance, calm. She looked like my mother used to when opening the door for me as a teenager every time I came home from a party exactly when I said I would. The apartment was chilly, as if the air-conditioning had been left on all day.

"What time is it?" I asked.

"Two fifteen."

"Something's happened."

I told her about working out the password and about Duke's account on SprintRun, about the path he jogged the night he was murdered and his consistent detours to my building. She turned away to face the artwork hanging on the living room wall, as if trying to distract herself. They were contemporary pieces, photo collages with textual interventions, paintings onto which materials had been applied for volume and texture, the kind of pieces people used to make at the time. Her silence was starting to grate on me. I had expected her to respond in some way to the turmoil gripping me.

"Does this make any sense, Francine? Say something."

"'Say something.' That's all anybody wants from me these days. To say something."

"Was he spying on me? Did he mention me?"

"You want me to say something? Maybe I didn't love him all that much."

She turned her head to face me again. As she emerged from the shadows, she looked more than ever like a big-chinned, slow-witted boy.

"Give me one of your cigarettes," she said.

I obeyed her. She placed the Camel in her mouth. When I made mention of lighting it, she grabbed my Jack Daniel's Zippo and studied it with a tormentor's dispassion. Objects lost life in her hands, becoming little blocks of material fated to awaken in her only a distant, fleeting interest. Francine could have been a replicant in *Blade Runner.* She handed me the lighter along with her first puff of smoke.

"Duke was cold. You know that. Next to him, I must have seemed warm. Devoted. But after he died . . ."

I didn't dare ask her to continue. I waited.

"I liked him a lot," she said finally, "really a lot, but I don't think I care as much as people think I should. After what happened. I mean, the role I'm expected to play. What people assume I should feel."

"I can imagine."

"Can you?" Another drag, another puff of smoke. "I think you can, actually."

"I can," I answered redundantly.

"Yeah. You can. When we look at each other, I feel like you understand."

All of a sudden, I was hit by my delayed exhaustion. My eyelids drooped and my neck fell forward, making my entire body arch in the armchair.

"You want to know why he used to spy on you at home, don't you?"

"I do," I murmured.

"You know why. He liked you."

"But."

"Platonic love, as they say? But I don't know if that was quite it. No, it wasn't exactly that."

"What a motherfucker."

"There are things we want to experience but never do. Because we can't. Because we won't let ourselves. Those things are little monsters born in basements. They grow. They wither. They become deformed. There's no way to know how the basement will affect them. But they stay there. The only thing the little monsters won't do is disappear. While we live, they live."

"Son of a bitch. Cocksucker."

"Sometimes, while we were having sex, he'd ask me to pretend—"

I leapt out of the armchair and took her face in my hands. Still sitting, she accepted my mouth as she had the lighter, like an object that could barely skim her curiosity. Like the customs of people from a planet that meant nothing to her. All at once, I became aware of my sweat and my grubbiness, of my greasy hands, my erection, and my crippling fatigue. I didn't quite understand what was happening. And I wasn't particularly proud of the little I did understand. It was uncharted territory, a thing new or seen for the first time that filled me with an energy that would be reserved for later. For a future moment that would be anything but tedious. I believed in the future. Francine led me to her bed to sleep. So long as that kind of energy existed, I thought before drifting off, so long as it kept surging in some of us, even despite ourselves, the world as we knew it would go on.

These days we know what awaited us, but I was in the dark like everyone else when I woke up that morning at the first signs of dawn. I brewed coffee in a tin pot and ate low-carb bread with cheese and honey. As soon as the sun dried off the dew and warmed the chilled earth, I went out for a walk, a habit I had developed since arriving at Emiliano's family ranch a few days earlier. He didn't know I was there, although sooner or later he'd connect the dots, seeing as I had brought up the subject of the ranch with him several times. No one knew I was there, not even my family, for whom I'd concocted the story of a research trip to the gaucho countryside. My fingers were stiff from the cold, and my lips cracked. Winter nights on those *cerros*, which was how the handful of people who lived in the area referred to the rocky slopes that dominated the landscape, were so cold and dark that it was easy to picture yourself floating around in outer space after the lights went out. But the sky remained clear, and as soon as I opened my eyes, I looked forward to the moment when I could work my knees on those slopes and trails scattered with rocks, packed into layers of jackets and hats, my lungs filling with pure air and my mind with silence.

I walked past the flea-infested shed and past the clothes-line heavy with sheepskin drying under the sun, then continued along the dirt road that led to the house of the nearest neighbor, Neto, an overgrown path you could barely make out beneath the green. Neto raised goats and sheep and, depending on the year, grew tobacco, corn, and watermelon. He showed up at least once a day, on motorcycle or horseback, in boots, knickerbockers, an ashen shirt, and a flat-cap, wanting to know if I was all right, intrigued by the presence of a woman alone in a cabin in the forest listening to music on her headphones beside the wood burner and wandering the hills in the morning, stopping now and then to admire creatures and plants. I'd told him only that I was a family friend and would be spending some time there, taking a break from city life. At some juncture, Neto would probably telephone Emiliano's parents and alert them to my presence, but it was already the tenth or eleventh day and not a question yet. Neto lived with his wife and his daughter, Diana. At fourteen, Diana's extraordinarily pale skin was already worn by the sun, and she had a very red mouth. She stood at what must have been nearly a meter and eighty centimeters and had long, vigorous thighs that ended in feet stuffed into knee-high, brown leather riding boots. She rode horses like a Hollywood princess, in a purple nylon jacket and blond hair tied back into a ponytail, hollering deep-voiced commands at the horses and dogs. She didn't speak to me. On one of my first mornings, when Neto had invited me over for lunch at his place—three kilometers away, on the other side of that valley at the bottom of which washed a small, lovely stream—I watched her sitting on a small bench in a corner of the kitchen, looking forlorn, shooting off text messages on her phone, rising only when her mother asked her to set the table or fetch something in the pantry. A van stopped there every morning to take her to public school in a town twenty kilometers from her house. How long until a boyfriend snatched her away to the city? Or would she choose to stay where she was, busying herself with the home life of a rural family, working the fields, vaccinating flocks? Could I join Diana, become her apprentice, her partner? Was the world ending for her, too? Did Diana also experience that feeling, did she think about it from time to time? Electricity had reached these people less than a decade ago. If my world were to end, would hers persist? Or would it be proven that we did in fact inhabit the same world? I couldn't shake the feeling that we would soon find out.

About two hundred meters ahead, I passed the orange grove where we camped on the last day of 1999. We had wanted that year to never end. And our desire that it last forever had been such that we didn't even notice the millennium turn. We were far from flashes and fireworks. It was Andrei who had announced, suddenly, to everyone's surprise, that it was already twenty after midnight.

After the orange grove, I veered off the path to Neto's house and took a trail that crept to the top of the hill and delved into the forest. In the pasture, small herds of sheep and goats chewed their food and busied themselves with transactions invisible to the human eye. It wasn't the first time I had wound my way there, but the paths forked, and the idea that it might really be possible to become lost in that place, never to be seen again, was increasingly compelling. Gradually, I left behind reference points that had become familiar to me from past hikes. A stone slab coated in a film of mossy water. A small gathering of precarious tombstones bordering the trail and engulfed by a dense green. An empty beehive box, its blue paint faded and peeling. Each step took me a little further from my family, my doctorate, my department colleagues, my handful of friends, of projects, my virtual existence. I reached the summit of a broad rock that provided an expansive view of the valley and of the hills that stretched into the horizon, punctuated with houses and barns few and far between, signaling the distant presence of humans in light-green pastures skirting dark-green woods. There were rocks all over the place, like the debris of an exploded planet. This was a mineral kingdom, in which men, animals, and plants were shown their place as creatures fleeting and interdependent.

I contoured the broad rock and descended the valley slope. After another densely wooded forest, I found myself on unfamiliar territory.

The vegetation native to the region around the ranch was made up in large part of hopbush, *Dodonaea viscosa*, a tree that thrived in poor soils and was always the first to grow after fire; and cambuí, *Myrciaria tenella*, whose fine branches composed curtains of unfurled roots in the hearts of woodland isles surrounded by pasture. The palmettos that had caught my attention fifteen years earlier were still there, growing around the edges of rocks and in rocky crevices. There were, to a lesser extent, yerba maté plants, auracárias, and butiá palms, familiar faces in those southern, rural landscapes. And bromeliads. Bromeliads everywhere. Around me cicadas shrilled and a bamboo grove creaked, still hidden by some curve in the path ahead. The growth thickened, and the trail narrowed so that to continue I was forced to break and part branches. The path ended suddenly in a suspiciously large glade that looked as if it had been cleared by people. In fact, in a corner I found the remnants of a dwelling, including a stone-and-mud wall nearly a meter tall. People had lived there decades ago. The thing that caught my attention, though, stood in the center of the glade. An already-dead, centuries-old cinnamon tree was dying the torpid death of trees, devoured by a young, bright, elephant ear fig. The two species seemed embraced in solidarity, yet in reality the fig tree was strangling the cinnamon tree in slow motion while the other parasitical plants, fungi, and insects proliferated in its trunk and roots, oblivious to the violence. That scene reminded me, among other things, of statues depicting battles or murders. Whenever I saw them, I would think to myself that they also moved at a pace too slow for the human eye, consummating acts of brutality in a time outside ours. I also thought of how beautiful that cinnamon tree was, even though it was dead. How beautiful they were as a whole. For months, the dead tree and the live tree would be one. For something to live, something, somewhere, must die. As I tried to direct my senses at the glade—at the phantasmagorical legacy of its former human inhabitants, the rugged scent of the soft breeze stirring the leaves, the buzzing and vibrations in that edge of the world, which offered itself up to me and only me, and made me who I was in that moment—a pale figure grazed my field of vision.

My heart raced. Moving only my head, I scoured the growth around me until my eyes fell on the creature. Among the trees, a white deer stepped gingerly, spying me from the corner of its eye, taking in my presence as I took in his. The forest didn't stir nor make a sound as it passed. The creature didn't pause, but moved slowly enough for me to watch him. He had reddened eyes. His white body was spattered with light brown spots, and his antlers were squat and black, covered in gray fuzz. I knew for certain what I was seeing. The deer drew away from me languorously. Its pale white dissolved slowly into the pitch dark of the native flora until, finally, it vanished. For a moment I wasn't sure what I should do. I followed the path he had taken, tried retracing his steps, but didn't see him again. He had descended into the depths of the valley, there, where the forest grew even thicker.

**ALSO AVAILABLE**

## THE SHAPE OF BONES

A young man wakes up at dawn to drive to the Andes, to climb the Cerro Bonete—a mountain untouched by ice axes and climbers. But instead, he finds himself dragged, by the undertow of memory, to Esplanada, the neighborhood he grew up in, to the brotherhood of his old friends, and to the clearing in the woods where he witnessed an act that has run like a scar through the rest of his life. From one of Brazil's most dazzling writers, *The Shape of Bones* is an exhilarating story of mythic power.

## BLOOD-DRENCHED BEARD

Atmospheric, both languid and tense, and soaked in the sultry allure of south Brazil, *Blood-Drenched Beard* first announced one of the greatest young Brazilian writers to the English-speaking world. Daniel Galera's spare and powerful prose unfolds a story of discovery that feels archetypal and builds with oceanic force.